THE FIRSTBORN

The Firstborn

House of Heaventree
Book 1

NICOLE SEITZ

Water Books

For those who endure.

PROLOGUE

Mister and Mrs. Flanagan always urged their kids to wear their hair long in front to cover up their naked foreheads. It wasn't that they were ashamed—it was that it was becoming too dangerous to flaunt the fact that they didn't carry the mark.

In those days, there had arisen a great G.O.D., the Global Operational Datalink. It was a satellite that controlled all communications—wePhones, wePads, computers, internet, gaming. It was supposed to be free, but nothing comes without a price.

After the Great Storms, communications were down for a year and a half, and society was crippled. Children who grew up with wePads in their hands didn't know how to learn or communicate in person. Socialization was awkward. Looking people in the eye. All of it. Dating was a fiasco. No longer could you research a potential mate for embarrassing photos online. You actually had to get to know the person...in person. Drivers were lost and went in circles as no one had learned to read a roadmap (nor were there any left), and GPS was no longer in service. So when the G.O.D. switch was finally turned on, the world was starved for electronic devices and ripe for what would happen next.

Within the first hour, 3.5 billion people connected. They all looked down, heads bowed before their devices in reverence. It was only in the second hour that anyone understood what they'd agreed to. A law clerk in Indiana actually read the Terms of Agreement before clicking "I agree." She noticed the fine print toward the end of the sixteen pages—the Herod clause. It stated that G.O.D. users would be permitted to access the wireless connection for free, assuming they "agreed to assign their first born child to the Global Union for the duration of eternity."

It was the beginning of the end. Millions attempted to fight the order, but the arguments didn't stand up in a court of law. Firstborns were handed over to the Global Union. They were given a small implant in their foreheads. It was a chip that connected them to G.O.D. automatically. These chosen needed no devices to research a topic or to calculate a difficult equation. Books were downloaded with just a mere thought. These special GU youth (GUYs) were as close to super humans as possible, and after a while, the G.O.D. added a clause that allowed individuals to sell themselves for free wireless access. Toys were made to glorify GUYs. Barbie now had a chip in her forehead. Anyone who had to use a handheld device was now a freak in normal society. Anyone who didn't receive the mark of the GU was an outsider, shunned—which made Flare and Cornelius Flanagan about as unpopular as two teens could be.

~ 1 ~

They must leave home now. They were told it's time—that they're finally ready. Flare and Cornelius Flanagan, ages 15 and 14, are standing at a crossroad, sent here by their parents. They described a narrow crevice between two buildings on Journey Street—it's only visible to those who have eyes to see and only stays open for those who believe. On one side is the dying bookstore, Leaf (for only a few need books any longer). On the other side, Chang's Chinese Food. A few steps back and across the street is Milo's Deli and Dry Cleaning, and at the end of the block, there is a busy intersection with a street light that flickers every time a car passes. This is where we find our teens, ready to crossover.

"She's barely in the ground two days," says Cornelius about his dog, Pepper. She died in his arms. He still tears up when he thinks of her, fresh grief wet as paint. "Couldn't we have waited a little longer?"

"Come on." Flare's red hair shimmers as she moves, her long bangs swaying, but not enough to reveal her naked forehead. It's the same color as her mother's though Mrs. Flanagan wears it pulled back, unafraid of what the world may say about her. She grabs their parents' note out of her brother's hands. "It's getting dark. We have to hurry."

A white unmarked van with no windows comes to the intersection, and the light above flickers. The van turns slowly and eases down the street in the same direction the siblings are moving. The brake lights come on. It stops. In moments, one, two, three, four teenagers step out onto the sidewalk in front of Milo's. They look around, hefting their backpacks on their shoulders.

"Are they GUYs?" asks Cornelius.

"Don't know," says Flare. She trains her eyes on them in the dim light. It appears to be two girls and two boys, but she can't see their foreheads. The neon sign at Milo's turns their skin a sickly green so that they look like zombies. "But they have backpacks like we do."

As slowly as it came to a stop, the van drives off again, leaving the four teens stranded there.

"Hurry," says Flare. "I want to get there first."

"Whoever is first will be last, and whoever is last will be first," teases Cornelius.

"Gee, thanks for that," says Flare, tugging on his arm. Her brother is smart. Freakishly smart. In fact, he's memorized most of the Bible. She clutches the note as they cross the street, trying to go unnoticed, but no good. They've been seen. "Here's the bookstore, and...there it is. Do you see it?"

"I see it but...we can't go in there," says Cornelius, stopping abruptly.

"Yeah, we can. Mom and Dad said this was it."

"But we won't fit," he whines.

"We have no choice," says Flare. She drops her book bag off her shoulder and lets it fall to her left side, dangling from her fingers. Then she turns sideways, pulls her stomach in, and squeezes into the dark crevice between the two buildings. She smells Chang's Chinese food, and her stomach rumbles. She hopes there will be food soon. Her whole family has been fasting for the day.

"Follow me," she tells her brother. The two edge themselves into the narrow space, feeling the wall behind them and in front, taking only one small sidestep at a time.

It's hot. Stuffy.

Cornelius starts to sweat.

"Stop, stop," he says. He puts his head back on the concrete wall and tries to get air in. He's always been afraid of the darkness. Always hated small spaces. He never could win at hide and seek because he was terrible at hiding. His throat would begin to feel like it was closing up if he hid under the bed or in the closet or anywhere dark and suffocating.

Like it is now.

It's happening again.

"Oh, God, help me," he says.

His sister breathes deeply for him, reminding him how. "Just in through the nose and out through the mouth, Corn. Come on, you got this. We're almost there."

Cornelius' heart is pounding through his gray hoodie. His scruffy brown hair is now plastered to his forehead. Flare is hot, too. She's wondering if they really are close. The thought crosses her mind that they never should have come. Maybe Corn isn't ready. All of a sudden, he yelps.

"Aaagh! Something touched me!"

"It's just me," says a voice.

"Who?"

"Me! Josh. Josh Dunwright. Who are you?"

"Cornelius Flanagan. And this is my sister, Flare."

"Flare Flanagan? Nice name," says Josh. He laughs a little.

Flare squeezes her eyes closed. "If you guys are done with this little meeting, can we get going?" she says through her teeth.

"Anytime now," says another voice.

Cornelius can't see anything, but there's no escaping. There's someone in front of him and in back of him. He's sandwiched in, stuck like a sardine. He begins the panting again. He feels his throat closing. He might as well be in a coffin. Coffin. Oh, Pepper. He starts to think about his dog again, buried in the back yard...

"Come on," says Flare. "Take a step to the right. Good. Now, one more. That's it."

Step by step, inch by inch, the six teenagers slide along the fourteen-inch wide crevice in pitch blackness. Then Flare says, "I'm here! Stop!"

Everyone stops in place and holds their breath. Everyone except Cornelius, who is beginning to hyperventilate. Are the walls closing in on them?

Flare feels the wooden door and searches for a knob. There isn't one. She pushes with all her might, but it doesn't budge.

"What's wrong?" asks Cornelius, feeling lightheaded.

"I don't know. It won't move."

"Turn the knob."

"There is no knob!"

"Hey, let's go!" says Josh.

"She's trying," says Cornelius. "Calm down." He listens to his own advice and starts to focus on controlling his breathing.

Flare is knocking at the door now. Frantically. "Come on! Somebody..." She's beginning to panic. She has people following her, people depending on her. She has to get this narrow door open.

"That's it!" she says. "Mom said that if we got stuck to remember the word of God. The narrow door. Isn't there a verse, Corn?" She knows her brother has a photographic memory and has memorized every Scripture...along with the Constitution, Declaration of Independence, and dates and stats of all the Presidents. Flare's always wished he could just be like other boys and play sports.

"Um...Make every effort to enter through the narrow door," he says, "because many, I tell you, will try to enter and will not be able. Luke 13:24."

The door clicks and cracks. "Amazing. It worked!" says Flare. "The door's open."

"Then go through it," says a girl from the back.

"I can't. It's opening toward me. You all have to move back."

They all squish together and grumble. They're tighter, strangers pressed up together as on a crowded subway train.

"It's not working," says Flare. "Corn, get the person in the rear to take three steps back. He turns to Josh's dark figure behind him, relays the message, and on and on it goes until the whole line of teenagers has successfully backed up in an orderly fashion.

Cornelius' heart is pounding. Flare pulls the door to her and takes a final breath before squeezing through the narrow space with her book bag.

"I think we made it. But I still can't see anything."

They all shuffle into a larger space, but stay close, huddled up. It's pitch black. Cornelius and Flare can sense everyone's presence around them as feet shuffle on the ground.

"Why is it so dark?" someone whispers.

"Wait. I've got a light," says Josh. A small flicker emerges from his fingers. He holds his lighter up and them moves it around the circle until everyone's face has been illuminated.

"Ow!" The light goes out when Josh burns his finger. He flicks it on again.

Flare sees his shock of blond hair and her heart flutters. He's not bad looking. *No. You're not here for guys,* she reminds herself.

"What do we do now?" asks Cornelius. "We only have one little light in all this darkness?"

"That's it!" says Flare. "A light in the darkness. What's the verse?"

"Job," says Josh, staring Flare in the eyes. "They grope in darkness with no light. He makes them stagger like drunkards."

The girls giggle. Everyone but Flare. "No, that's not the

one, thank you," she says sarcastically. "Corn? Come on. What is it?"

Josh curses under his breath. He must have burnt himself again. The flame goes out. They all stand in silence until Cornelius says slowly, "You, Lord, are my lamp; the Lord turns my darkness into light."

Suddenly the room fills with light. And Flare and Cornelius can't believe their eyes.

$$\sim 2 \sim$$

Three days earlier...

Cornelius is playing catch in the backyard with his 15-year-old dog, Pepper, when she drops the ball and starts panting more than usual. He watches her back legs wobble and give out on her. "You okay, girl?" Cornelius bends down and lifts her 30 pounds of tan fur. She's not as stout as she was when she was younger. He carries her inside and puts her in her bed near the window. "Flare!" he hollers. "Come quick! It's Pepper."

"What's wrong with her?" his sister asks. She's only a year and a half older than him, and although she isn't a grown up, it's all he has at the moment. Their parents have gone out for a while and won't be back for another twenty minutes. Cornelius usually revels in the freedom of being left home alone, but now he wishes they were here.

"I don't know what's wrong. She's weak all of a sudden. Breathing heavy." He pets his best friend and kisses her on the head. "Get Dad or Mom!"

"They're not here!" Flare says testily.

Pepper pants in her bed. Cornelius sits down on the wood floor beside her and studies her eyes. They look different, scared. She seems to be looking to him for help. He offers her water from her bowl, but she refuses it. He closes his eyes. He starts to pray. *Oh, please God, help Pepper. Help her get well.* "It's okay, girl." The dog doesn't seem to get better. Instead, she begins yelping, and her eyes open wide with fright.

"Quick! Call somebody!"

"We don't have a phone!"

"Then go grab a neighbor! Do something!"

Pepper's yelping increases, and Cornelius and Flare watch helplessly as she finds the strength to scurry out of her bed, slip two feet across the hardwood floor and crawl up into Cornelius' lap.

The boy, terrified now, begins to pray out loud. "Father God, please help Pepper. She's such a good girl. Please, God, help her!"

The dog begins to calm in his lap as he strokes her. Her panting slows. *Is this good or bad?* She's having trouble breathing. Gurgling sounds come out of her as if she's drowning. She buries her head up against his warm torso.

She stops fighting.

"No! No!" Cornelius knows she's dying now. There's no doubt in his mind. He knew this day would come at some point, but he wasn't ready for it. It's too late to do anything for his loyal friend, so in a moment of steely desperation, his prayers change. "Oh, God, please take Pepper to heaven. Please, God, in the name of Jesus, don't let her suffer. Please take her quickly! Don't let her suffer!"

The air is charged with something. Emotion. Sadness. God. He isn't sure. Cornelius is in a state of alarm mixed with grief and helplessness, the depths of which he's never experienced before. He is aware of his own pleadings coming from his lips and soon becomes aware of another voice. It's his sister. She's reading Scriptures beside him.

"The Lord is my shepherd, I shall not want. He leadeth me to lie down in green pastures..."

Tears pour from Cornelius' face as he feels his little dog lose her struggle. It's impossible to believe that the dog he's loved all his life, the one who has loved him unconditionally, who's slept with him every night, is gone. That he'll never see her again. Her body is still warm, but there's no movement, no breath. Her eyes are empty and dark. Time seems to have stopped, and he isn't sure how long he's sat there, but he tells his sister to say goodbye before her lingering spirit vanishes forever.

Flare leans over and feels the dog for a heartbeat and breathing. There is none. "Oh, girl, I love you so much. I'm sorry. I'm so sorry." She sniffles and wipes her face on her shoulder.

"I'll never forget you," cries Cornelius. "Never."

They don't move for a very long time, brother and sister side by side, holding their beloved friend. Has she gone to heaven as they had pleaded? Will they ever see this dog again on the other side? The kids aren't sure about the theology of the whole thing, but they know something for sure. They have truly loved and been loved by this animal. If that isn't heaven worthy, they aren't sure what is.

When Mom and Dad come home, the dog is back lying in her cozy bed, and the children are crying in shock beside her.

"What's going on?" Mom says. "Oh. Oh no, Pepper." She comes in and looks at the dog. She bends down and touches her gently to be sure she isn't there. She reaches over and rubs her head one last time. Then she looks at the kids, utterly destroyed. "Oh, sweet babies," she says. Then something strange flies into her eyes. Something like fear. Mom turns around to look at her husband who has quietly closed the door behind him. He wears a look of severity like a mask. He doesn't look like himself. "She's dead?" he asks them.

The kids nod. They watch as their father seems to crumble, weak-kneed. He rubs his chin then the back of his neck.

"Does this mean—" says their mother.

Dad nods. "Yes. It's time."

$$\sim 3 \sim$$

Having all made it through the narrow door, the teenagers are standing in a magnificent garden. "Whoa..." says Cornelius, his eyes trying to adjust to the light.

"You can say that again," says Josh. All six are turning around in circles, trying to take in the enormity of the vaulted atrium, the tropical trees and flowers situated around benches and little hideaways. Cornelius longs to go find a place to sit and hide out for a while. With a whir, the roof begins to recede, revealing a glass dome. The stars are starting to shine.

"Is this the school? Is this it? We get to go here?" asks a girl with long, iron-straight blond hair and glasses. The teens face each other for the first time in the light. Cornelius and Flare stand arm to arm. Although she's annoyed with Josh for being so cute, Flare knows it's polite to introduce themselves officially. After all, it looks as if they'll be going to school together.

"Hey, um, so I'm Flare," she says. "This is my brother, Corn."

"Cornelius," he corrects.

"I'm Atlys," says the blonde girl. Her glasses are two red rectangles on her cheeks.

"Nattie," nods an Asian-American girl with short cropped hair and shaggy cut-off jean shorts.

Josh's left dimple creases as he smiles at Flare. "Josh. We've met."

Flare thinks about how well he fills out his football jersey.

Everyone is silent for a moment, waiting for the other kid to speak up. His skin is dark brown with near bluish tones. Flare thinks he has a nice jaw and broad shoulders. "What's your name?" Josh asks him.

"You mean you don't know each other?" asks Cornelius.

"No," says Josh. "They just picked us up and brought us here."

"Marcus," says the boy. He rubs his chin and continues to stare up into the sky and around the garden in amazement. "Wow. I've never seen a place like this."

Flare picks up on an accent. "Where are you from?"

"I'm from Africa," he says. From Sudan. I've been in America for three years."

Josh sucks on his burnt thumb then says, "So, what are we supposed to do now? Wait here? Go somewhere?"

All of a sudden, the ground shakes. Flare holds onto Cornelius.

"What's that?" says Marcus. "Earthquake?"

"I don't know, we're—we're moving!" says Josh.

The teens lock onto one another as they descend into darkness. The floor is moving them down, down, down...

$$\sim 4 \sim$$

Two days earlier...

The seconds tick by on the grandfather clock, the final countdown.

"Flare, I'm scared," admits Cornelius.

"Me too."

The silence between brother and sister is thick and black like the air around them. Cornelius and Flare lay side by side on their sleeping bags in the living room. It's their last night at home before having to leave for boarding school. They don't know why they have to go. Their school was perfectly good. It was at home. They made good grades. They had good friends.

"This all seems to be happening so fast," says Flare. "I mean, Mom and Dad said they were planning to send us there all along, but why didn't they tell us?"

"Probably because we'd have a fit. Like we did tonight," says Cornelius. He rolls over and hugs his teddy bear. He's had Beary since he could remember, and although he's way too old for stuffed animals, he doesn't think Flare will make fun of him tonight. Tonight is different. Desperate.

A tear rolls over his nose silently as he remembers his

dog, Pepper, who would have been sleeping a few feet away in the corner if she was still alive. "I miss Pepper," he says.

Flare is quiet. Then she says, "I don't want to leave home. I don't want to leave Mom and Dad. I'm going to miss them so much." Her voice cracks, and Cornelius can hear she's crying now. This unnerves him. She's the stronger one.

Although they have their differences occasionally about who's going to weed the garden or compost the trash, or how Flare takes too long in the shower and lets all the water run out—normal brother and sister things—Cornelius hates to hear his sister cry. His heart hurts for her. It makes him strong. For her.

"It's going to be fun. Think of it," he says. "You and me, off on our own, no parents to tell us what to do."

"The school will tell us what to do."

"Yeah, but we'll be independent. Like Stephan and Lora are now."

"Stephan and Lora have sold their souls to the Global Union. They're tracked everywhere they go. They have thoughts downloaded for them. You really think that's independent?"

Cornelius is quiet. His blood chills with the thought of his old friends. Finally Flare says, "I just worry about Mom and Dad. It's not like just one kid is going off. Both of us are leaving. How is Mom going to stand it?"

"How is Dad going to stand it?" says Cornelius. "Who's he going to play soccer with or teach physics to?"

"Who's he going to yell at to clean our rooms?"

Cornelius smiles in the darkness.

"But did you see his face? There's no changing his mind. For whatever reason, he believes completely that this is where we need to be. He loves us, Flare. They love us. Can you even imagine what it will be like to send us off on our own after being so overprotective? This is going to kill them tomorrow. Just try to be brave for them. Try not to cry and make it harder."

"I can't promise that," says Flare.

"Yeah," says Cornelius. "Me neither."

The two of them stop talking. For the next several minutes, all they can think about is what they're going to miss most about home. Cornelius thinks of his mother's hugs and how she comes in to kiss him goodnight...still, after all these years. He thinks of her spaghetti and meatballs. How Pepper would jump up and steal one off the table.

Flare thinks of Dad's face as he would sit in her room and try to talk with her about friends, boys, the state of the world. None of it came easily, but she always was touched knowing how hard he was trying to stay connected to his ever-changing teenage daughter. It's funny. Try as she might, on the last night in their home with the whole family together, Flare can't remember a single bad thing that's happened here, although she knows there were plenty. Even the groundings and discipline seem sweet to her now.

In an instant, she has a bit of understanding. She can see her whole life with her family from beginning till now, and how it was all to prepare her for what's coming next.

Whatever is coming next.

$$\sim 5 \sim$$

When the ground is still again and the lights come up, it's so bright the teens have to shield their eyes. They're standing on a stage at the end of a large gymnasium. People in the bleachers begin to clap and cheer.

For us? Are they cheering for us? Cornelius wonders. He also wonders how fast he can run home if he leaves right this second.

"Welcome to Heaventree," says a baritone ringside announcer, "a true faith-based preparatory school. Not only where students master academics and arts, but where they become physically fit, mentally fit, and most importantly, spiritually fit to handle any test of faith. On behalf of the faculty and administration of Heaventree, let me say we are honored and excited to have each of you here with us tonight. You are welcome guests, brothers and sisters in Christ."

Cheers and whistling. *Deal! Deal!* yell a few in the crowd.

"Thank you, thank you. I am Mr. Deal. You are correct, fine sirs and ladies. Now. Let's get on with matters. Look around you, folks. None of us has the mark in our foreheads. We're all outsiders. But in this place, we're one.

Each of you belongs." A microphone moves so quickly in front of Flare, she nearly jumps. "What is your name, Miss?" Flare looks at the man. He is thin, tall, wearing a shaggy black haircut and a t-shirt that says HEAVENTREE.

"Flare. Flare Flanagan," she says timidly.

"Welcome Flare Flare Flanagan," he teases. "Now. Flare. It is indeed true that whoever is first will be last and whoever is last..." he holds his microphone out toward the crowd.

"Will be first!" yell the people in the bleachers.

Flare is anxious. How did they know about that conversation? Were they listening to them? Watching them? Is this Big Brother? Is Mr. Deal really a GUY?

"Exactly right. Last will be first. Our Lord and Savior Jesus Christ was, of course, talking about servanthood and the saints that enter heaven in the end days, but for our purposes, you and your friends here, the last ones to arrive at Heaventree, will now become the first. You six are the new heads of our six houses here at Heaventree. Flare, you are now the head of the House of Flare." The audience erupts.

Mr. Deal puts the microphone in front of Cornelius's face. "Your name?"

"Cornelius."

"The House of Cornelius," calls the announcer. More clapping. The man moves down the line of teens announcing the Houses of Josh, Atlys, Nattie, and Marcus.

"Each of you will be in charge of one-sixth of our student body, that is, each house will have 24 students.

You will each live under the same roof and will have different but important tasks to complete and, of course, responsibilities."

Cornelius tugs on the man's shirt and whispers, "Excuse me, sir. There must be some mistake. I—I can't be the head of a house. I'm—that's just not me. I'll just go in my sister's house."

"There's no mistake, son," says the man, quiet now, leaning in Cornelius' ear. "Our God is sovereign. He's chosen you to be a leader. Trust me on this."

"And now for the rest of you anxious students," he says returning to the microphone, "you will find six boxes by the doors. On your way out, please select a ticket to choose your house. Ladies, you may choose either the House of Flare, of Atlys or of Nattie. Gentlemen, please select either the House of Cornelius, the House of Josh or of Marcus. Each house has 23 tickets. As soon as the tickets are gone, that house is full, and you must choose another house with an available ticket.

"Now. God willing, you will all choose wisely." He waits until the murmur quiets down.

Cornelius feels a sense of dread. Why does he have to be separated from his sister? Are they really not going to be able to stay together? He grows panicky and feels an anxiety attack coming on. He longs to be lying on the living room floor again, hugging Beary with his sister close by.

"All right," says Mr. Deal. "I won't hold you any longer. Off you go!" Above the movement of bodies on the risers and the hurrying of feet and excitement of voices, the man calls out, "We will meet outside these doors on the Great Lawn. Find your leader and stand with him or her and your housemates. The fun is about to begin!"

~ 6 ~

Cornelius notices his name on the box as he heads for the door of the gym. *House of Cornelius* it reads. He looks at the people putting tickets into the box slot. They're choosing his house? Why are those boys choosing his house? Don't they know he isn't a leader? His face feels flush. He's about to walk out the door when a hand grabs his arm. He turns, stunned.

"Joe!" he says. Joe was his friend in homeschool. He's known Joe Powers since second grade, ever since Joe's family moved here from Washington. He reaches out and hugs his friend tight, so relieved to see a familiar face; he doesn't know what to do. "It's so good to see you! I didn't recognize anybody, and I was about to—"

"I chose your house," says Joe. "I hope that's all right."

"All right, are you kidding me?" He feels a new lightness in his step. Joe is solid. He and Cornelius have never been terribly close, but that's only because they had several good guy friends. "Hey, have you seen anybody else?"

"Nah," says Joe. "Just you and me. Well, and Amy Feinstein is here."

"Amy?" Cornelius feels sick to his stomach. He's not

sure what that's all about. Amy is, well, he's never paid much attention to her. She only came to homeschool last year and seemed shy. She's pretty in a weird kind of way. Well, yeah, pretty, Cornelius thinks. His face gets hot so he rubs his hair off his forehead.

"For a while, I thought I was the only one who had to go to this school," says Joe. "I had no idea about it until a couple days ago."

"Me neither," says Cornelius, his curiosity piqued. Why would Joe's parents spring this school on him too? Why not tell them in advance? The two boys walk out into the sunlight on the Great Lawn, but are quickly ushered underneath a huge shelter with picnic tables. He finds a table with a sign on it that reads *House of Cornelius* and has to pass *House of Flare* to get there.

"Corn," says Flare.

Cornelius looks at his sister. She seems nervous and alone even though girls are starting to crowd around her. He wants desperately to talk to her, but the crowds are settling and he needs to get in his place. He's the leader of the house, after all. Flare reaches her hand out to him, and he low-fives her on the way. She grabs on and tries to hold his hand then lets it go as he moves past.

His heart hurts.

He misses his parents. He misses his dog. He misses his house. He misses his homeschool friends. His sister is several feet away, but now he misses her too.

Cornelius feels nervous, but at least his sister is nearby and he has a buddy, Joe, at his side. Mr. Deal, the announcer, has no microphone this time. Instead, he walks in front of the picnic tables, facing the six houses and their throngs of students.

"Before we go any further, I'd like to pray. Please join me." Cornelius and Flare catch each other's eyes. When she bows her head, Cornelius follows and looks down at his sneakers. He's still looking to his sister for what to do in situations. He wonders how he'll be able to make decisions without her. And if so, what kinds of things will he have to decide?

"Dear Heavenly Father, we thank you for every student that is here today. Lord, we know that there is no accident that anyone is here, that you have known about this divine appointment since before we were ever born. Thank you for your love for us, thank you for sending your son Jesus to die for us so that we may truly live."

Cornelius feels himself beginning to relax. He closes his eyes.

"God, I pray that you would open the hearts and minds of our students, give them a desire and passion to know and follow hard after you, and Lord, please give us your special protection as we go into this school year. Refine us, Lord, and make us ready, prepare our hearts, minds, spirits and bodies for what you have called us to do. In Jesus' name we pray. Amen."

Cornelius opens his eyes and looks around at all the new faces. It'll be all right. They're all brothers and sisters in Christ, right? Jesus is why they're all here. And school. It's just like his old school, really, except they're away from home and his parents aren't here. It'll be just like that camp he used to go to in the mountains. Only longer.

Right?

A group of grown-ups joins Mr. Deal in front of them. They're a motley assortment, mismatched in every way. "Ladies, gentlemen, you are now organized into your houses. Look around you. These will be your new friends. Family even. Look to each other. Help each other. Watch out for your brothers and sisters. I know you don't know each other very well, but that will change very quickly. To help you in your coming year, each house has been assigned a house mentor. I, myself, am the mentor for the House of Cornelius."

There is a murmur in the crowd around Cornelius as Mr. Deal nods his way.

"Not only does each house have a house mentor, each will be associated with an area of learning. Cornelius," he turns his attention directly to him, "as I am the head of the History, Current Affairs, and Biblical Prophecy Department, those will be our areas of expertise."

Yes! History. Cornelius loves history. He loves dates, things he can memorize. What a lucky break for him to have Mr. Deal and History in his domain. Maybe he can do this, after all.

Mr. Deal goes on to introduce the rest of the faculty members. The House of Flare will be mentored by Miss Carmine, a tall young woman with dyed, nearly purplish hair, wearing a paisley lavender dress. She, of course, is the head of the Visual and Performing Arts Department. Flare is beside herself. She grins at Cornelius. How can they have paired them so well? Did they know that Flare was an aspiring fashion designer? Did they know she doodled over every book she read?

Josh throws his arm up in the air to get his housemates to cheer, *Ar-nold! Ar-nold!* when it's announced that Coach Arnold will be mentoring him and they'll be focused on Physical Education and Athletics. Josh is already dressed for the part, wearing a football jersey. Many of the boys around him appear the same.

Professor Moss, the Head of Science, a pale round woman in Birkenstocks who doesn't bother with makeup comes forward to claim the House of Atlys. Atlys hugs her and pushes her red glasses up on her nose. The House of Nattie goes to the Math and Logic Head, Dr. Vollmer, a dark-skinned man with a distinct nose and no-nonsense khakis. He has two ball point pens in his pocket. He and Nattie can't look more different. But maybe she's into Math, thinks Cornelius.

"And last but not least, Madame Dubose, our head of Languages and Literature department will mentor you, Marcus, in the House of Marcus." A wafer-thin woman with wispy black hair comes forward. She says something in a foreign language. French? No. Spanish? Not quite. Marcus answers her in his own native language and goes to shake her hand.

There are smiles and nods all around. Cornelius looks about him and begins to notice a pattern. The students seem to have picked houses with similar people in them. Was that an accident? Was it stereotypical, people choosing houses because of how people look? But no. It's not that. They don't look alike in appearance, there's something else. Is it possible people can seem alike in spirit? If so, Cornelius is hopeful his house will be united in spirit. They have to be. He hates conflict, detests guys who pick fights like Ezra Keenan with the missing tooth who lived down the street. He used to steal Cornelius' wePad...until he sold his soul to the Global Union and didn't need one anymore.

Cornelius looks at Joe and tries to smile, but then everyone is ushered into a door. House by house, student by student, they find themselves in a dark tunnel, sort of like a subway station. Except instead of a high speed metro train, there's an antiquated wooden cart, and another, and another, and another, all connected.

"Just pretend it's a roller coaster ride," says Mr. Deal, standing at the first car.

He opens the door. Everyone is deathly quiet.

"For reasons we will share with you shortly, we will be spending this new school year a little further away from here. Six of you to a car, please, don't skip anyone. Make sure you have your housemates around you. Keep your hands and your feet inside the car at all time, and whatever you do, don't look down. No, I'm just kidding. This isn't a roller coaster. But it is necessary to get where we need you to go. So...vámonos! Safe travels. I'll see you when I see you!" Mr. Deal steps into the car and then Miss Carmine, Coach Arnold, Professor Moss, Dr. Vollmer and Madame Dubose all file in with their small suitcases.

Mr. Deal nods at Cornelius, so he follows suit. One by one, the doors to the cars are opened, and the students cram into the small, old wagons. As soon as all 144 students are on board, the cars start moving. What's propelling them to go forward, Cornelius doesn't know. All he knows is that it's beginning to get darker and darker, and the tunnel is getting smaller and smaller, and oh, how he hates small, dark places. A little lantern flickers in front of him as the car shifts and shakes over the rails. All he can think about are bats. Bats are probably in here. Of course, they are. He feels his throat closing up. Joe leans over to him and says, "Where are we going?"

"I don't know. This is pretty freaky, though."

"Yeah. Pretty freaky."

"I—I don't think my mom and dad knew we were going to go somewhere. Did yours?"

"No," says Joe. "How will they know where we are?"

Both of them are wondering what they've gotten themselves into. What if their parents were tricked? What if this is actually a group of human traffickers and all these kids are going to be sold into slavery in some foreign country? He's heard his parents talk about it before.

Cornelius' heart is pounding now, and his face runs with sweat.

They ride in silence deep under the earth, or so Cornelius thinks, for what seems like a very long time. How long is this tunnel, anyway, and why do they have to be underground? Cornelius turns around to look for his sister, but it's no good. It's too dark, and this old coal train has too many cars. His heart stops, thinking maybe she didn't made it. If Flare doesn't go with him, he'll have nobody. Nobody!

Worse, what if she *has* made it and she's going to be sold into slavery too!

He grabs at his neck, but there's no shirt there, just skin. *Breathe,* he tells himself, *breathe.* But he can't.

Cornelius blacks out. When he comes to, he has a headache, and the truth comes rushing back to him. He fainted on his first task, riding a coal car. Some leader he's going to be.

~ 7 ~

It's all Flare can do not to call out her brother's name. She knows he's dying, almost literally, in this dark tunnel. Why do they have to do this? Where are they going? How long will this take? Why didn't they tell them anything about this trip before? Why didn't Mom and Dad say anything about it?

Breathe, Cornelius, breathe, she says with her mind, hoping somehow her thoughts might travel to her brother telepathically. Oh, who is she kidding? *Please, God, help my brother in this tunnel. Watch over him and protect him. Amen.*

For as long as she can remember, it's been her job to watch over her brother. Well, hers and Jesus' job. But claiming that Jesus wasn't watching over Corn while they were jumping on their beds and he missed by a foot and broke his ankle—well, she learned she couldn't make Jesus a scapegoat for things she was perfectly capable of preventing. Her parents would often put her in charge of her brother, blaming her when he whined or got hurt. Sometimes it was her fault, no doubt, but others—well, it seemed like she took the fall for just about anything that happened to Cornelius just because she was older. And things were always happening to Cornelius.

First of all, his name was Cornelius. Flare had to wonder what her parents were thinking when she named him after a great-great uncle who fought in the war. Yes, he had saved his platoon by jumping on an explosive and sacrificing himself, but still. Cornelius just was not cool. Corn is what Flare called him. Not Corny, not Cornball. She didn't make fun of his name; she protected him with his nickname, although Corn never saw it that way. What could she say? Corn was his own person. He didn't much mind what people thought of him. In some ways, Flare admired him for that. If there was one way she wished she could be like her little brother, it would be that she wouldn't care so much what other people thought of her. Sometimes it was debilitating, especially with not having the GU mark and all the abilities and perks that came along with it. She tried to come off as totally cool, nonchalant and not easily rattled, but deep down she struggled.

Flare's mom once sat her down and told her that it mattered only what God thought of her, not what anyone else did. It made a lot of sense to Flare, but every now and again, that same insecurity reared its ugly head.

It's beginning to do it again. As the coal cars rattle over the tracks through the darkness, Flare begins to worry. She worries about where they're going to wind up. She worries about being the head of the House of Flare, whatever that is. She worries that her little brother is no longer under her protection. She thought she'd have him underwing and be able to look out for him, to guide him—

well, if she was honest, to boss him around. She knows she's bossy, she does, but Corn doesn't seem to mind. It works for both of them really. Her bossing him is just her way of caring, of staying in control of what happens to him. Corn is all she has here. Her parents are still at home, and they probably don't know where they are now. She doesn't know any of these people. She has no friends.

As she tunnels deeper and deeper for what seems like an hour or more now, Flare feels her heart nearly racing out of her body, and she knows her brother may be on the verge of a heart attack. Flare wants to scream out for him to see if he's okay, but she bites her lip instead. She doesn't want anyone to think she's weird or anything. After all, everyone seems to be handling this trip to the unknown a whole lot better than she is.

This, too, worries her.

After rambling for what seems forever, Flare begins to see a light at the end of the tunnel. White-green light grows larger and larger until Flare's car and the ones before her emerge into fresh air. She smiles, and a sense of relief washes over her. The coal train is surrounded by blue mountains in the distance and green leafy trees. Sheltered by branches, everyone's face and hair is bedazzled by sunlight. Over the grumbling of the wheels on the track, Flare can now hear the people in her car talking. The girl beside her is turned around and listening to the other two behind them. Flare sits up straight and cranes her neck to see if she can spot her brother in the second car from the front. She can't see him. *Don't panic*, she thinks. She prays again.

"Where do you think we are?" asks the girl beside Flare. She's petite with sandy blonde hair, wearing a simple pink dress with t-shirt sleeves. Something about her looks familiar. Flare wonders if it's because she's been beside her this whole time. Then, no, it's more than that.

"You look...have we met before?" asks Flare.

The girl looks down at her hands. "I don't think so, no, but I sort of know your brother."

"Corn?"

The girl nods. "We were in the same group at home-school. My mom taught gardening. And sometimes we came to your house church."

"You did? Right. Oh, wow. Small world."

The Flanagans had been holding church for a few families ever since their church had closed down years ago along with all the other churches, synagogues, temples, mosques and other houses of worship. With the majority of the population selling their soul to the GU, there were few people of faith left and certainly not enough to pay for the cost of buildings.

Flare notices fear in the girl's face. "I'm Flare. What's your name?"

"Amy," she says.

"Amy, I really don't know where we're going, but I'm sure we'll be fine. Okay?"

Something lights up in her. The fact that someone here has come from their school and their home church, aside from Flare and Corn, makes her feel better slightly. She knows this girl is younger than she is, and that brings out some sort of maternal instinct or something. She'll watch over Amy. Flare was completely out of sorts not having her brother to care for and now...now she has a temporary replacement. To anyone it would sound crazy, but it occurs to her that God knows her so well. Having this girl in her house will aid that deep longing Flare has inside to nurture.

Thank you, she prays silently. Her eyes fill with tears at the thought of how much she is loved. Then she leans back, and for the first time, tries to enjoy the ride.

~ 8 ~

Cornelius has never been so happy to see trees and ground and grass in his life. He gasps, wondering if he held his breath the entire bumpy ride. He watches as Mr. Deal and the other teachers exit the coal car in front of him and wave for them to follow.

Quietly, the 144 new students file out and hoist their backpacks over their shoulders. Some stretch or turn around, looking at future friends and the new place they've come to. There's a small sign tacked to a tree trunk. *HEAVENTREE* it reads. *That's it?* Cornelius wonders. It's pretty casual. He could have hand-written it himself. Mr. Deal takes his place by the sign and puts his hand up to get everyone's attention. "Gather round," he says. "Gather round.

"Welcome, friends, to Heaventree. I do hope you enjoyed your ride. You may have noticed we left our main campus a while back. You are now about to enter Heaventree's new campus. It's, uh, well, it's hidden. We're hidden here. We have to be." His face goes dire for a moment, then he clears his throat and puts his hand on the tree beside him, the one with the little school sign.

"This tree, here, is our mascot, if you will. It's a most special tree. Can anybody tell me what kind of tree it is?"

Silence is all around except for the song of a couple birds far away and the breeze blowing through leaves. Cornelius feels a burden to speak, being that he is one of the group's leaders, but he doesn't know the answer. He wonders if the other heads of houses, specifically Flare, feel the same awkward weight. Atlys, the pretty blond girl with red glasses raises her hand.

"Yes?"

"Is it a fig tree?"

"It is a fig tree. Excellent. Now. Can anyone tell me why we might have a fig tree at the entrance to our new campus?" says Mr. Deal.

Cornelius feels a surge in his throat. He raises his hand and Mr. Deal acknowledges him.

"Because a fig tree is Biblical? Sir?"

Mr. Deal smiles. "It is in the Bible, yes...can you tell me where? Well, it's mentioned many times, but there's one in particular. One that has to do with the seasons."

Cornelius closes his eyes for a second before answering. He wants to be right. "Now learn this lesson from the fig tree," he says. "When its twigs get tender and its leaves come out, you know that summer is near."

"Excellent. Keep going."

"Even so, when you see all these things, you know that it is near, right at the door. Truly I tell you, this generation will certainly not pass away until all these things have happened. Heaven and earth will pass away, but my words will never pass away."

"Good. From the book of Matthew," says Mr. Deal. He puts his hands over his face and rubs. "Friends, does anyone know what that passage is about?" His voice is much more somber. There's no more bravado. His eyes scan the group. Cornelius thinks he knows what it means, but he wants to give someone else a chance. Doesn't want to look like a showoff. "You. Yes? Marcus, is it?"

Marcus begins to speak, his accent drawing the listeners closer to understand. "Jesus was talking about things to come. He had just told his disciples that he is coming again someday and that the end of times is coming then too. Just as we can see that summer is coming by looking at the signs of the fig tree, we can know that Jesus is coming back, and that the world will end as we know it, by looking at the signs around us."

Everyone is quiet for a moment. Mr. Deal's eyes glisten. "That was just right, Marcus, thank you, my friend." Mr. Deal lifts his tattered blue Bible and holds it up. "Heaven and earth will pass away, but God's word will not. This is good news for us. We should take comfort in the fact that God's word never changes. That God, himself, never changes. Even when times bring trouble, and Jesus promises we will have troubles, I want each and every one of you to know where to turn. How to stand firm in your faith. Friends, not to put a damper on things, but the world is changing, even as we speak. Take a look at this tree." He reaches out and touches a leaf. "Leaves," he says. "Signs of the times. War, famine, disease, persecution, earthquakes, tsunamis, evil. Summer is near, and it's not the kind of summer you students like to dream about."

He smiles and everyone lightens up a bit.

"Seriously. Heaventree is a special place. We are hidden from the world for a short while. We are here to prepare you for what is to come. Boot camp for your soul, if you will." He smiles again, and turns on his showy announcer voice. Cornelius had become fond of the authentic, more vulnerable one he heard in those few moments. He's silently grateful and humbled that this man is to be his mentor.

Cornelius turns to look for his sister and notices she's walking toward him. "There you are," she says, hugging him. He needed that hug so badly. He didn't know it, but this strength of being on his own is wearing thin. He puts his head on her shoulder for a brief second. Flare smells like home, like Mom and Dad, like Pepper. Tears overwhelm him, but Cornelius sniffs and pushes them back. She smiles at him and puts her hand on his back as they prepare to enter.

"Once you enter this door, know that our fall session has commenced. You are safe here. You are welcome here for as long as you want to learn. But you will find we are not your typical school." His voice trails as he walks past the tree and into an archway covered with vines. One by one, the students follow in single file onto the new hidden campus of Heaventree.

~ 9 ~

Upon entering the vine covered archway, Cornelius and Flare are dumbstruck. They've never seen anything like it. Standing in front of the fig tree, they saw none of this. But how? Heaventree is a city. Sort of. But it isn't any kind of city they're used to. "It's like the whole world, right here," says Cornelius in awe.

"I know," says Flare. The whole group of kids is silent and reverent. It's as if each building represents a different country. The architecture is astounding. A Gothic stone building with details like Notre Dame Cathedral, another wood framed structure like a Japanese tea house, a bright yellow Victorian with carved spindles, and a huge masonry building with tall ionic columns and a rotunda on top. There's even a very modern chapel made of angles and tall peaks of metal and glass.

A woman slips beside Flare and Cornelius and leans in close to whisper to Flare.

"Isn't it marvelous?" she asks.

Flare recognizes her as the head of fine arts, her mentor, Miss Carmine.

"Each building was funded by a benefactor, and

obviously, each benefactor was from a different part of the world. Look at how every building seems to take you someplace far away."

Cornelius speaks up. "But I don't understand how I didn't see this from standing outside the gate. Did you see it, Flare?"

Miss Carmine says, "Mr. Deal told you this place is hidden."

"But how?"

"Let's just say, there were many who took part in the building of Heaventree. Some of the best minds in and out of this world. Don't question it just now. Just be glad we have a secret place to learn here."

"Why so secret?" asks Cornelius. "Mom and Dad never mentioned we'd be going so far away."

"Your parents knew you'd be in good hands when they sent you here. We take that very seriously at Heaventree. We've been planning for this day for a long time."

At that, Mr. Deal gets everyone's attention and invites them to enter the Main Hall, a massive Gothic revival building with stained glass.

"You'll be eating your meals here," he says, his voice nearly echoing in the vast ceilings. The students gawk and crane their necks to look at the wood trusses arching over them. A wall of stained glass covers one side of the building, a stone fireplace flanks one end, and the back is a wall of clear windows that showcases a view of a deep blue lake and gardens. The long rectangular tables are arranged in rows with spaces so one can walk in between. There are no chairs, only benches the length of the tables. At the far end is a food court. After a mass blessing, the students are instructed to help themselves.

Silverware and plates clink. Kids rush to a long buffet with salad and chicken and rice and brownies. After having fasted for more than 24 hours now, Cornelius eats until he feels sick. He has his sister at his side, Mr. Deal as his mentor, and this amazing, most beautiful campus he's ever seen. Suddenly Cornelius is filled not only with food, but with an overwhelming gratitude that he's here.

It's almost enough to make him forget for a moment the longing he feels for his parents at home.

Almost enough. But not quite.

~ 10 ~

Flare is sitting on top of a picnic table behind the Main Hall. She stares out over the lake, her elbows resting on her knees. After a few minutes, her head falls to her chest. She's exhausted. It's been a very long day, and evening is coming fast. She's happy for Corn that he and Joe have found each other. They're off throwing a football down near the lake. She lifts her head and watches them for a little while then stares into the blue ripples. A duck lands and bobs along. Alone. Like her. Flare startles when someone says her name.

It's Miss Carmine, her mentor. "May I sit with you?" she asks. Flare nods.

Miss Carmine climbs her long thin frame up on top of the picnic table next to Flare. She curls her lavender dress beneath her knees. She's a young woman in her early twenties, with purplish hair pulled back loosely in a ponytail.

"It's beautiful out there, isn't it?" It's rhetorical. Flare understands that. Miss Carmine gazes out across the water and then looks at Flare. "I'm going to be your mentor," she says.

"I know," says Flare.

"Are you an artist?"

Flare doesn't have to think about it. Yes, she's an artist. Maybe not the traditional kind with oil paintings and realistic portraits, but she considers herself an artist. A master doodler. Drawing helps solidify things in her brain. She can listen to a message or lecture, and the doodling firms the concepts. It's as if she hears better through the end of a pencil. But Flare decides to be a little cooler about it.

"I guess so," she says. "I like to draw."

"Me too." Miss Carmine smiles and doesn't go on about it. Flare likes this about her. "I know you're all tired. Tonight, we'll have you staying in Chizoba Hall. In a minute, I'd like you to help me round up your housemates so we can get them situated."

"Ok," says Flare.

"And there's one more thing." Miss Carmine bites her lip and looks out of the water once more. "I have letters for everyone. Letters from your parents."

Flare's eyes open wide and she sits up straight. "Letters from...Mom and Dad? Really? Everyone?"

"As far as I know, yes. But, Flare..." It seems Miss Carmine is having a hard time getting her thoughts out. "As a house leader, I wanted you to be the first one to get your letter. I—well, I have to prepare you—"

"What?" Flare interrupts, nervous now.

"No, just that sometimes people get more homesick when they receive a letter from home. Whatever is in those letters, as leader of the House of Flare, you're going to have to be a backbone of sorts. If some of the girls...I don't know...get sad or upset, you've got to be strong for them. To help them through."

Flare thinks of little Amy, Corn's friend. "Of course," she tells Miss Carmine. "Can I have mine now? I mean...may I?" She's trying to remember her promise to her Mom and Dad to use her best manners.

Miss Carmine steps down. She walks to a brown bag on another picnic table. Flare hadn't noticed the bag before. Opening the flap, Miss Carmine rifles through it until she pulls out a letter.

"My brother, Cornelius, does he have one too?"

"I believe so." Miss Carmine stands above her and hands her the envelope. "I can stay if you want me to."

"No, that's okay," says Flare, looking over the carefully drawn letters of her mother's impeccable handwriting. *Flare Flanagan*, it reads. Her stomach twists. Her name looks beautiful in her mother's hand.

"All right," says Miss Carmine. "But if you need me, here." She reaches around her neck and unhooks a necklace. She hands it to Flare. It's a pretty heart locket with filigree. "It's a short-wave radio. Very short wave."

"No way."

"It is. And it's undetectable. Doesn't connect to the G.O.D. at all. All you do is press that little button on the side if you need me. Got it?"

Flare puts the necklace on and presses the button. She says, "Miss Carmine. Come in Miss Carmine."

The woman nods at her and holds up her own matching

necklace. "See, I heard that," she says smiling slyly. Then she walks away to leave Flare alone with her mother's words.

Dear Flare,

I hope this letter finds you and your brother well. Please know how much your father and I love you both. I know you were surprised that we were sending you to a new school, and I admit, two days was not a lot of time to prepare yourselves mentally. I hope you will forgive us for this, but we told you a small story. You see, your father and I have known for quite some time that we would send you to Heaventree. We just didn't know when that would be. Until three days ago.

Flare, this is Dad here. I just borrowed the pen from your mother so I could explain this in my own words. This is not easy, and I wish we'd been able to speak about it face to face, but we couldn't. What I want you to know first is that God is never surprised. He knows in advance what things will take place. In the Bible he gives us many prophecies and prophets. He is merciful in this way. He desire is to communicate with his people to tell them when they are doing wrong, or how to prepare for difficulties.

As you know, our country and our world is the most restrictive it has ever been for people of faith. These are hostile times. No longer can we meet in the church buildings. No longer can we speak of our faith in Christ without enduring some scorn or hardship. People have lost their jobs, their homes, their livelihoods, and it is only going to get worse. We've known this for a long time now. Any regular reader of the Scriptures will be able to see that things will only get worse. However, Jesus is our hope and our redeemer. We have no reason to be afraid of what will come.

So now about me. The prophet Joel said that in the end

times, God would pour out his spirit on all people and "sons and daughters would prophecy, young men would have visions, and old men would dream dreams." This has happened to me. I do not claim to be a prophet, but something astounding began to happen to me just before you were born. The Lord began to give me dreams. These dreams were very minor at first. I once dreamed my fingertip was red and swollen, and the next day, I received a deep paper cut on that finger. I thought it was an interesting coincidence. Nothing more. But then it continued. I dreamed of my father in a car wreck, and a call to my mother confirmed he'd been hit the day before. Words and numbers found their way into my dreams and the day after, those words or numbers would be important in the news or otherwise. At some point, I told God that he had my attention. I believed he was communicating to me though my dreams. He was training me, if you will, to pay attention to my visions. And then, I experienced a dream so real, so vivid, I woke up sweating and wrote it all down. Mind you, this was before you were born. We weren't even expecting a child yet.

In the dream, there was a dog. There were also two children and your mother and me. We were happy. Very happy. And then the dream turned darker. The dog died, and immediately we were in danger. I won't go into specifics here, but let's just say, it became clear to me that the children had to leave for safety. It was even given to me in my dream a man's name and a place for them to go.

Flare, apparently I am not the only one who had that dream. Upon connecting with this man, he let me know that he had received many, many letters from people from all over the country. People who had had similar dreams or visions as mine.

Indeed, the man existed. Indeed, the school was already in the works as benefactors have been preparing for this dark day for many years.

Our dog, Pepper, came to us as a stray soon after my vivid dream. She was a tiny puppy who had curled up behind a planter filled with pepper plants at our back door. I didn't think about the dream much after I wrote it down, but then you and your brother came. When you were small children, it occurred to me. I pulled out my journal. I recognized you as the children in my dream, and Pepper—she was the dog.

When she died the other day, your mother and I knew it was time. The dream was becoming a reality. We have hoped this day would never come, but it is here, and I need you to be as strong as you can for your brother. Know how terribly we miss you, but that we are comforted knowing you are in a safe place.

Know that there is no safer place than in the arms of our heavenly father. Our faith in Jesus Christ as our savior brings us immeasurable joy no matter what the circumstances. Even though we miss you, God is with us, and he will be with you, too, always. Keep him close. Never turn from him or his ways. Read his word daily. Digest it until it has become a part of you. They are living words that transform the inside and will allow you to persevere through any trial.

Flare, this is Mom again. I want you to know I never had any of these dreams or visions, but I respect your father and trust his walk with the Lord without a doubt. I, too, know you are in the right place, and I am comforted. Don't worry about me. I will be sad for a while, but I will survive. I expect you to do the same. One more thing. I believe one of you, either you or Cornelius, or both, may have your father's "gift" of visions or dreams, of God communicating to you in this way. If and when such a gift is discovered, don't be scared of it. Rest in the fact that God loves you so much that he would speak to his children to warn you of events to come.

God willing, we will see you both soon. Take care of your brother. Take care of yourself. Learn everything there is to learn, and know that you are LOVED!

With deepest love in Christ forever and ever, Mom and Dad

~ 11 ~

Corn. Flare has to go find Corn. Did he get a letter from Mom and Dad too? She stuffs the letter in her backpack and throws it over her shoulder. Corn was down by the lake with Joe...but where is he now? Where is everyone?

Flare runs back into the Main Hall and sees some men cleaning up the tables and floors with brooms and washcloths. "You lost?" one of them asks.

"I guess so. Do you know where everybody went?"

"Over to Chizoba Hall," says the man. His black hair is tinged with gray. "Must have been about five, ten minutes ago. Where were you?" he teased.

"Just reading, I guess." Flare reads his nametag on his gray suit. "Thank you, Mister...Remley."

"Ain't nothing. Just here to help." He smiles, then turns back to his work, whistling. Flare takes off out the front of the building and down the path, backtracking toward the entrance. She turns left between two buildings. Aside from some lights, the sky is mostly black now. Why didn't she ask exactly where it was? Why did she think she'd be able to figure out?

Oooooh, Chizoba Hall. That's why. Flare stops, and her

mouth drops open. This must be it. Chizoba Hall is a massive structure that would fit in well on the savannahs of Africa. It's made to look like a gigantic treehouse, but the trunk of the tree is big enough to fit her whole house back home. The upper floors creep out like branches, climbing and twisting. Flare rushes to the front door and enters the foyer. Tall grasses and plants line the walls and colorful patterned rugs cover the floors. A woman is standing at a counter.

"Excuse me. I'm looking for the other kids."

"House of?"

"Flare. I mean, I'm Flare Flanagan. But do you know where the House of Cornelius is? I really need to see my brother."

"Everyone is in the atrium, I believe, unless they've sent them to their rooms. In that case, House of Flare is on the third floor and Cornelius is on seventh."

Flare thanks her and runs through doors. The atrium is huge, reminding her of the great garden she first entered through the narrow crevice on Journey Street. How long ago that seemed. Was it only hours? No one is there, so she rushes to the elevators. She passes a man sweeping the floor. He turns and catches her eye and smiles. Is that the same guy she met in the food hall, Remley? No, it can't be. That's impossible. He could never get here in time.

Flare is beginning to panic, though she isn't quite sure why. She'll get to Corn and see that he's okay. She remembers what Miss Carmine said, that her housemates might need her. That she may need to provide emotional support after they receive their letters, but all she can think about is her brother. And their parents. And how they're in danger of some sort. What danger is she and Corn escaping? Why couldn't their parents come with them?

On the seventh floor, Flare knocks on every door until she comes to the last room, 712. Joe answers the door. There are two bunk beds that look like hammocks hanging in trees. Joe's face is sullen. Corn is sitting on an animal-skin-patterned beanbag near the window. He's holding his letter.

Flare passes Joe and goes straight for her brother. He doesn't move, so she crouches to the floor and sits beside him, saying nothing for a minute. Finally, she utters, "Mom and Dad?"

He nods. His face looks red.

"Me too." She moves to grab his letter but he pulls it away.

"I just want to see if it's like mine."

"I'm sure it is." Corn folds it and puts it in his back pocket. Then he stands. "Apparently Pepper was part of some...I dunno, plan. God's plan, I guess. I'm supposed to go talk with my housemates now. That's what Mr. Deal said. You should too. Joe, here, got a letter from his dad. He says he moved here from Washington after having a similar dream. Only he didn't have a dog that died. Instead, it was his grandma."

"Oh, I'm sorry," says Flare.

"Yeah, well," says Joe. "I'm just a little weirded out. How could so many people have dreams? How could they all know to send us here?"

"God," says Corn. "It's prophecy. He speaks through

people. He tells us in advance what He's going to do. The Bible is full of examples."

"Well, I'm no prophet," says Joe.

"Me neither," says Flare. "I gotta go find my house-mates. I'm pretty sure I failed my first test in leadership. Right?" Flare musses the hair on her brother's head and says, "See you in the morning? You sure you're okay? I'll be on the third floor if you need me."

"I'm good," says Corn.

Flare forces herself to believe that. Then she runs down the hall to the elevators. She's thinking about Amy now, wondering what dream or vision brought her here. Surely she knows by now and is freaking out on the inside, just like Flare is.

~ 12 ~

"Rise and shine, happy campers! The Lord has made a glorious new day. This is your fearless host, Mr. Deal, and do I have a deal for you. Meet me at eight a.m. near the front gate of Heaventree. Get up now! That is all."

Cornelius groans and puts the pillow over his head. Joe grabs his pillow and throws it at the speaker on the ceiling. "Is he going to do that every morning?"

"Probably," says Cornelius. He can't help thinking about his mother. She woke him up every day of his life, and now...this? A lump forms in his throat. He feels the edges of his letter in his hands. He held it close to him all night long, needing something, anything, to remind him of home. Beary falls to the floor, but Cornelius grabs him and sticks him under his covers before Joe notices.

Taking it upon himself to be the leader of the House, Cornelius gets himself ready and knocks on all the doors of his housemates, urging them to get down to the Main Hall for breakfast. After each is accounted for and fed, they walk as a group out to the front gate. He waves but keeps his distance as he watches Flare trying to rally her straggling girls.

"Can you imagine having a house of girls?" said Joe. "You'd never be on time. They have to fix their hair and, well, whatever girls do."

"Yeah," says Cornelius. "Try sharing a bathroom with one your whole life." He says it to sound cool, but all it does is make him miss home and how things used to be.

The six houses form clusters of kids on a large lawn. People stretch and yawn and wait for Mr. Deal and the other teacher mentors to arrive. When they do, they are all dressed in jeans or shorts, no dresses for the ladies. They each have hats and tool belts around their waists—Mr. Vollmer, the Math professor, looking the most uncomfortable with this dress code change. Mr. Deal is holding a large scroll in his hands.

"Good morning, folks. Well done. I hope you ate a hearty breakfast for today is a big day at Heaventree. To-day you each get your first assignment. But first, let us pray." Heads bow. "Dear Heavenly Father, we thank you for this day. We thank you for our rest and daily bread, and now we ask for your blessing on what we are about to undertake. Father, let us always work as if we are working as unto you, the Lord, and let our hearts find joy in our work, knowing we have a purpose to fulfill. Watch over and protect each student at Heaventree, and fill each of its teachers with wisdom and understanding. It's in Jesus' Holy name we pray. Amen."

The group of kids is completely silent. Cornelius is anxious.

"We've been planning for your arrival and for this day for a very long time," says Mr. Deal. "Now, you know

I've mentioned that we are not a regular school and this morning, you have a most irregular assignment. I hold in my hands...plans for each of your houses. You, my friends, will be building your own houses."

Cornelius feels his blood pressure rise. His heart is beginning to pound. He hears a girl ask, "What do you mean, building our own houses." It's Atlys. "You mean, like, actually building, like with wood and nails and all?"

"Like with wood and nails and all," says Mr. Deal. "Yes."

"But we don't know how to build," says a boy on Cornelius' team.

"You don't, no, but you will when you have your plans and your mentors work with you. I realize many of you have never lifted a hammer, but nonetheless, this is what your first task will be. Not only that, but you have one week to complete the houses."

"One week?!" the whole crowd erupts and panics.

Mr. Deal puts his hands in the air, and all eyes are on the plans.

"Oh ye of little faith," says Mr. Deal. The group settles slightly, but there are still whispers and murmurs. "In a moment, I will give each of your heads the plans to your house. You will each have access to the same supplies, enough for all six houses. Each plan is similar but slightly different. You are to stick to the plan. Do not veer from the plan. Are we clear? Good. Now one last thing." Mr. Deal looks at his fellow teachers then down at his feet and back again. He seems to be staring directly at Cornelius.

"You will have one week to complete your houses from the time I give you your plans. Fail to complete your task in time and you're entire house will sleep in tents in this very field for the duration of your time at Heaventree."

"What?"

"That's not fair!"

Mr. Deal's normal jovial expression turns stern. "Are we grumblers or are we men and women of God? You have one week, ladies and gentlemen. Time is of the essence. Heads of houses, come and get your plans. The clock begins...now."

~ 13 ~

Cornelius is staring at the big mound of supplies in the middle of a green field. He's holding a rolled up blueprint in his hand, and the paper is beginning to stick to him as he sweats. His team gathers around him. Each boy wants to see, but he's getting claustrophobic. "Can everybody back up a minute?"

He knows he sounds testy, and it's not what he wants. "Sorry, I....everybody, have a seat. Right there on the grass."

He unrolls the plans and lays them on the ground. The first page shows what the building should look like when it's done. The others break things down piece by piece.

"It looks like a...a barn!" says one of the boys.

"A barn? We've got to live in a barn?" says another.

"Wait a minute, guys," says Cornelius. "This is probably a lot simpler than a massive house with a lot of floors and rooms, am I right?"

"Yeah, probably."

"And we have one week to build it, right?"

"I guess so."

"Then let's be thankful we only have a simple barn to build."

Everyone is silent while Cornelius looks over the plans. He's amazed that everyone is actually looking to him for leadership. *I'm the man with the plan,* he says to himself. Then he smiles at how goofy he is. He breaks out in a sweat again, thinking about all these boys in one week's time having to sleep in tents, all because he can't lead them through this task.

"Does anybody here have any building experience?"

"I built a doghouse once," says a boy named Henry.

"I helped my dad build a playhouse in the backyard," says another named Simon.

"Good," says Cornelius. "So you've actually used a hammer. You two will be my go-to guys for construction, okay?"

The boys smile and sit up straighter. Cornelius notices how pleased they look, and it makes him feel good. *Hey, if I can delegate each task, and everybody has something different to focus on, this thing might actually get built.*

A piece of Scripture floods him. "'Unless the Lord builds the house, the builders labor in vain.' So who needs to build this house?" asks Cornelius.

"God," the boys say in unison.

"Right. We're no different than Noah when he was given the instructions on how to build the ark. You think he'd ever built an ark before? I don't think so. He just followed the instructions and had faith that God was with him. We have to do the same."

"Isn't there a verse about building your house on a good foundation for when the rains come?" says Joe.

"There is," says Cornelius, grateful that Joe is helping him inspire the group. "'Therefore everyone who puts these words into practice is like a wise man who built his house on the rock. The rain came down, the streams rose, and the winds blew and beat against that house; yet it did not fall because it had its foundation upon the rock.'"

Evan, a small boy sitting cross-legged in the back of the circle of kids, raises his hand silently.

"Yes?" says Cornelius. He feels odd. He's not a teacher. No one has ever raised his hand to ask him a question. Cornelius feels himself blushing.

"Sounds like we should pray then," says Evan. "Would you like me to pray?"

"Sure. Go for it."

"Dear Heavenly Father. We thank you for this green grass we sit on. We thank you for this beautiful day. We thank you for the great opportunity you have given us to build a house in one week. Lord, we do not know how to build, but you do. Please be our rock. Please be the foundation we build upon. Give us the strength and the courage to do our very best. And don't let any of us get hurt. Oh, and please give courage to Cornelius, our leader. Help him to be confident, not in himself, but in you. Amen."

Cornelius is choking up. He's never heard someone pray for him before that wasn't his mom or dad. He almost feels like he's strong enough to do this now.

"Evan?" he says. "How would you like to be in charge of prayer?"

"Got it, sir!" says Evan, saluting. Everyone laughs, and the air seems lighter.

"Guys, it's time. I guess we need to go get some tools."

"Already done, gentlemen." Cornelius turns around and sees Mr. Deal standing there with his arms crossed, smiling. "You'll find your tools right over there by the number one. Everything you need is there. Saws, hammers, even the materials to build. All your wood etcetera. I suggest the first thing you do is get some math wizards to measure out and stake the property."

"Cool."

"Come on!"

The boys get up and run over to the sign with the number 1 on it. The students in the other houses are already in their places and scurrying around, trying to get started and figure out how.

"Mr. Flanagan," says Mr. Deal.

"Sir?"

"I like your style so far. The boys need someone they can respect. You've already directed them to God. Keep that up, son. It'll serve you well."

"Yes sir."

"And Cornelius?"

He looks at him.

"Is there anything you need from me right now?"

Cornelius thinks. "Ten more weeks? Or how about a hundred more workers?"

Mr. Deal smiles and rubs his head as they walk toward the land chosen for the House of Cornelius.

"I can't do anything about the time, but keep doing

what you're doing and I just bet you end up with a hundred more workers someday."

Flare looks at her plans for the House of Flare and crinkles her nose. The sun is in her eyes. She watches some of her team members staking out the property with string. She looks again at the plan. "It's a barn," she says to herself. It's so plain. She grabs the pencil behind her ear and starts sketching on the first page. "What if we made the front look like this?" She adds windows and a front porch. It's starting to come together. She even knows what colors she'll paint it. If only she had some colored pencils right now, but oh well. She can add that later.

Amy comes and finds her. "Flare, I was over there and, well, some of the girls are starting to complain already. They say it's too hot. And they don't know why we have to do this."

"So we have some place to stay," says Flare.

"I know, but they say they don't know why they can't just stay in Chizoba Hall. It's really nice there, and there is plenty of room."

"There is plenty of room but—" she rolls her plans up roughly and scowls. "Never mind. I'll go tell them myself."

Flare walks up to the girls stringing the stakes. They're sweating. There are three girls doing all the work. The others are standing there watching them or watching the other teams work.

"What are you all doing?" says Flare. "Don't just stand there. We're wasting time."

"Well, you haven't told us anything to do."

"Yeah, and it's hot. And we're thirsty."

Flare is annoyed. She can't stand complainers. She raises her eyebrows. She opens her plans and looks at the second page. "Holes. It says we need some holes dug." She walks over and grabs a tool that looks like it digs holes. "Here. We need someone to measure out where to put the poles. Then we dig the holes...and then we put concrete in the holes and then the poles down in there." She holds the pole digger out but no one grabs it. "Come on," she says. "Somebody's got to do this. Look. The House of Marcus is almost done with its hole-digging."

"Why don't you do it if you're so eager?" says Marley, a girl with freckles and hands on her hips. She smirks and elbows the girl next to her.

Flare is hot. Hot inside and out. She's failing. She's being humiliated in front of the people she's supposed to be leading.

"Fine," she says. "I'll do it myself." She hurries over and starts measuring where the holes should be. Amy runs over to her.

"Let me help."

Flare doesn't look at Amy when she says thanks. Her eyes are welling up with tears. She misses home. She hates being here. She hates being in charge of Marley. All she can think about is Marley disrespecting her. Yeah, well, she'll show her. She jabs the hole digger down into the ground, squeezes with all her might and then pulls up the earth. Her arms ache. Man, that was hard. And she only got two inches of soil?

"How deep does it say these have to be?" she asks.

Amy looks through the plans. "One and a half feet."

Flare looks at all the places she's marked for the holes. She can't do it. There's no way she can do it all. "I'll help," says Amy. "We'll take turns. And I bet the others will come over in a few minutes. You'll see. It'll be all right."

Flare sniffs and tries to stay strong. But inside she's worried. Very worried. She wonders where Miss Carmine is. Why isn't she helping? Does she expect a bunch of kids to do this all on their own? She thinks of using her necklace to contact her and ask her exactly why they have to build these stupid barns anyway. But she's not in a good mood and afraid she'll say the wrong thing, so she chooses to keep her mouth shut. For now.

Then she jabs the earth again, deeper this time.

~ 14 ~

By day two, Cornelius can't get out of bed. He feels as if he's been run over. His body is heavy. He lies there with his eyes closed as Mr. Deal's voice comes over the intercom in Chizoba Hall.

"Good morning, Heaventree! Rise and shine, there is much work to be done. This is day two of our house-building week, and let me remind you of what is at stake here. The house that has not raised the roof, so to speak, by Saturday evening will be sleeping in tents in the out of doors."

Cornelius opens his eyes and remembers where he is. His dog, his parents, leaving home, the narrow door, the long ride over, all of it comes flooding back to him.

"You. Yes, you. Did you enjoy your cozy bed last night? Don't you just love Chizoba Hall? Ah, all the comforts of home. Well, enjoy it while you can."

Cornelius is now sitting up, legs thrown over the bed.

"Oh, I almost forgot. The rankings! Here is how you did on day one. The House of Marcus is in first place, tied with the House of Josh. These houses have already set their poles in concrete and begun building the trusses. Well done. The houses of Cornelius, Atlys and Nattie are neck and neck for second place as they, too, have poured their concrete and set their poles. However, no trusses have yet begun. This brings us to last place, the House of Flare, which has dug all its holes but failed to pour all of the concrete footings. Ah, ladies, I do hope you can recover from this setback. Concrete takes a while to set. I'd get busy on those trusses if I were you. Remember friends, do everything as if unto the Lord. Let him partner with you for his ultimate glory. This is the best advice I can give. And so, this is...Mr. Deal, signing...out!"

Joe grumbles and sits up on his hammock. "Dude, I'm sore. Everywhere."

"Me too," says Cornelius. He rubs his eyes and says, "But today could be even worse."

"Yeah, probably." He laughs a little. "It's kinda cool though."

"I know. We're building a house."

"Yeah. Cool. Sounds like your sister might be sleeping in a tent soon."

Cornelius doesn't like the sound of this. If they were in the same house, they'd be in this together. As it is now, he can't help her. Can he? Sure he can. He'll find her at breakfast and figure out what's going on. He can't let Flare —and Amy—sleep outside.

The Main Hall is buzzing with kids. They've only been together for a couple days, but already friendships are being forged. They're working hard as teams, in the trenches together, surviving together. It's not an altogether unpleasant feeling, Cornelius has to admit. He feels as if his day has a purpose. A mission.

He sees Flare in the buffet line and goes to talk to her.

"Hey, Flare." He smiles, and she seems relieved to see him.

"Hey, Corn! Great job yesterday. I'm so happy for you. Looks like you guys are doing great."

"It...it's not easy, but it was only day one. I'm sorry to hear you were in last place. It's only the first day though. It's anybody's game, right?"

"We won't be in last place for long. We just had some...personality issues yesterday. Nothing permanent. I was up most of the night figuring out what went wrong. For one thing, my mentor is M.I.A."

"Miss Carmine?"

"Haven't seen her. Everybody has a grown up to help but not us. Well, we don't need her anyway."

"There you are." Flare's face turns as red as her hair when she sees Josh walking up with his plate of food. "I got you a seat over there."

"Be there in a second," says Flare.

Cornelius raises his eyebrows, but Flare acts as if she doesn't notice. "Josh is going to give me some pointers. Isn't that nice of him?"

"Yeah, nice," says Cornelius. Inside, he feels weird. He was going to help his sister, but now it looks as if she doesn't need him. But it's good she's getting help. "Okay, well, I'll see you outside later. Good luck!"

His sister walks over to the table filled with members

of the House of Josh. Several of the girls in her house are there, too. Cornelius looks over toward the window and sees his house all sitting together. They look so small. They look...like he does. Cornelius smiles as he sees heads bow and Evan beginning to lead them in prayer. He hurries over in time to say, Amen. He has a hard time eating because he's so nervous and excited for the day, but he knows he needs the energy. He's laughing at a joke when someone touches him on the shoulder.

"I just wanted to tell you, great job yesterday." It's Amy. His stomach lurches.

"Thanks," he says. "You too." Then he realizes how stupid he sounds. She's in last place! "I mean, well, I know you guys worked hard. You'll catch up today." His face feels like fire. Is he blushing? He turns away but can still see her face in his mind. Her blond hair. Her green eyes. Her smooth skin. When he turns back around, she's gone.

Cornelius tries to finish his pancakes, but he can't seem to get in another bite. He's done.

Cornelius and his buddies are hammering trusses that will support the roof. He has a station manned by Callum and Eric where all the sawing and cutting of wood takes place. Another station where the trusses are laid out on the ground like huge puzzles, and then he, Joe, and a few of the others hammer everything into place. His arm is so sore, he can barely lift it. Every time he wants to quit, he looks over to the other houses and sees trusses built and ready to go. He can't come in last place today. He can't. He looks over at his sister's house to see how they're doing. Not so great. Some of the girls are working on filling the holes with concrete. Some others are trying to figure out how to cut the wood to be the right size and cut on the right angles. They haven't even started hammering anything together yet. Where is Miss Carmine? They need all the help they can get.

"I gotta talk to Mr. Deal," Cornelius tells Joe.

"Got it. We're good." Joe has sweat pouring down his temples. Cornelius looks over his team, his house, and swells with...something. Gratitude. Yeah, gratitude. He's glad he came here. Glad his mom and dad found out about this place. In just a couple days, he feels like his confidence has grown exponentially. He feels like a man, even though he's only fourteen.

There he is.

"Mr. Deal!" Cornelius runs over to him. He's talking with Mr. Vollmer and Ms. Moss.

"Cornelius, what can I do for you? You guys doing okay?"

"Yeah, we are, but my sister's house," he turns and looks at them, "well, they're still going pretty slow. I think they need some help. Do you know where Miss Carmine is? Flare hasn't seen her since yesterday, and well, she's supposed to be mentoring her, right?"

Mr. Deal looks over to Flare's group and hesitates. He looks back at his peers, and Cornelius notices a very suspicious glance between them. It's quick, but he knows what he saw.

"Miss Carmine. Yes," says Mr. Deal. "Well, I believe she may have been detained for the moment, but I am so glad you brought that to my attention. Tell you what. I'll mentor the both of your houses today. All right?" Mr. Deal musses the hair on Cornelius' head and sends him back. "Be there in just a few minutes. Let your sister know help is on the way."

Cornelius walks back to his group but turns around to see all three teachers standing closer with their heads down. What's going on? How and why was Miss Carmine detained? Did she go somewhere? Is something wrong?"

"Flare." Cornelius stands beside his sister as she tries to adjust the miter saw. "Come here."

"Amy, will you look at this? I'll be just a second. It's supposed to be two inches." Amy takes over and Flare walks with her brother out of listening distance. The sound of hammering is all around, a head-throbbing cacophony. Cornelius thinks he'll hear it in his sleep tonight.

"What's up?" asks Flare.

"I got you some help."

"Who? Josh already gave me some pointers. We're doing okay."

"No, you're not. Flare, look. You guys are way behind. Look at everybody." The two study the other groups and Flare bites her lip. Tears flash into her eyes but she sniffs and makes them go away.

"Well, at least Marley's working today. She was so rude yesterday."

"What did you do?"

"I didn't do anything!"

"No, I mean, how did you get her to work?"

"Oh. Simple. I made her feel important. I told her I couldn't do this without her. That she was really smart, and there's no way we could get this done without her on the team."

"And that worked?"

"Yeah. Pretty simple, huh? I remembered that issue we had with Annelle. Remember that girl with the long curly hair who came to our house church? She was so mean to me all the time. Mom told me she was jealous of me for some reason. She told me that she just didn't feel special. If I just let her know how special she was—which isn't lying, because God thinks of us that way—the problem would end. It worked then, and it's working with Marley. Look at her over there! She hasn't stopped, and she's even making the other girls work harder."

"Wow," says Cornelius. "That was inspired. Mom is so...wise. But you're still lagging behind. You need these trusses finished today and the framing to start."

Flare's shoulders fall, and she takes a deep breath.

"I talked to Mr. Deal about Miss Carmine. He says she's detained, whatever that means, and he's going to mentor you till she's back."

"Really? Thanks, Corn. You did that for me?"

"Yeah, well, I don't want you sleeping outside forever. You're a terrible camper."

They both smile, remembering sleeping in the back yard with their dad. He loved to camp, but every morning, they'd find Flare back in her cozy room with stuffed animals all over her.

"I just like a nice warm bed." She elbows him. "Well, thanks. But you better get back to work."

"Right." Cornelius is about to turn and rejoin his house when he stops. "Listen. I don't know really what I saw, but I think I saw a weird look on the mentors' faces when I mentioned Miss Carmine. I don't know what's going on with her, but...well, maybe you ought to pray."

Flare reaches up and feels her necklace. "She gave me this to keep in touch with her if I needed to. Said it's a short-wave walkie-talkie. Should I try it?"

"Why not?"

Flare hesitates. Then she moves it to her lips. She

presses the little button on the side and says, "Testing, testing. Miss Carmine, this is Flare. Can you hear me?"

She lets go of the button and hears nothing but static.

"Come in? Miss Carmine?" More static. "Maybe it doesn't work," she says.

"Or maybe she's out of range," says Cornelius. "Maybe she left Heaventree."

"Why would she leave Heaventree? She's supposed to be my mentor. What would be so important that she would leave?"

"Don't know. But I'm guessing prayer is definitely in order. Look. Listen to everything Mr. Deal says. He's really smart. Ask him all sorts of questions."

"I will."

"And Flare." He grabs her arm. "Don't come in last today."

They stare at each other, neither blinking, and then he turns and heads for his hammer.

~ 16 ~

Cornelius wakes to the sound of rain drumming outside his window. For a while he thinks of his backyard, how the rain would drip over the trees and grass, how the roses his mother planted would glisten blood red in the spring. The playhouse in the corner, the patio with handprints he and Flare made when the concrete was poured. All his childhood memories. He opens his eyes.

He's in Heaventree, far from home. It's raining outside. Raining. He sits up. How will they work in the rain? He puts his hands on his forehead and thinks of the tasks at hand. He imagines slick tools and sloshing around in the mud. The rain will slow them down, but they can't afford to miss a day. They won't finish building in time.

Cornelius walks to the window past Joe who's still asleep in his bunk. It's barely daylight. The sun hasn't fully come up, or if it has, it's hiding behind the clouds.

Father, will it rain all day? he prays. The sky gives him his answer.

Mr. Deal hasn't delivered the wakeup call yet so he has a little time. Cornelius goes to his bunk and lays back down. He pulls out a little flashlight from his pack and drags his letter from his parents from beneath his pillow. He reads part of it again.

We sent you there so you would know what was coming. So you'd be ready for anything. So you would survive the coming tribulation—yours and Flare's and the rest of your generation. For us, it is here, at the door. Our trial begins now, but we're ready. In many ways, the Lord has been preparing us since before we were even born. No matter what happens, know we were prepared. Remember who you are, once the son of thieves, now a child of God, saved by grace through Jesus Christ, gifted with visions, prophecy, memory, heart. Use everything you've got. You and your sister and the others are the hope of the world now.

There's more, but he doesn't want to read it again. He's stuck on the "son of thieves" part. He has no idea what that means. Does he mean that since we're all sinners and only saved by Grace that we're all sons of sinners or sons of thieves? He doesn't know. Something doesn't sit right. Dad couldn't be talking literally about him and mom. They're not thieves. What could they possibly steal?

He shakes his head. He's sure it means nothing. He folds the paper and tucks it back under his pillow. Outside, the rain still falls. Cornelius thinks of crying. He misses his parents. He misses Flare. He still sees her, but it's not the same. Nothing is like it was before. He could cry, easily, but he won't. He's got to step up as a leader. Today's going to be the toughest day yet.

Flare is already awake. The rain woke her up an hour ago. Will it ever stop? She's never felt this much pressure in her life. She has 23 other girls who are all in the same boat with her. If they fail at building their house, they all sleep outside. She hates this. And she hates that Miss Carmine has totally dumped her. How can she do this without a mentor? It's not fair. The other houses have help.

She turns over and pulls the pillow over her head. There's no way they can get the trusses up today. She closes her eyes and tries to envision herself standing up on top of the framing and all the other girls lifting a heavy truss up to her and Amy and whoever else they need up there. In sunshine, it's hard enough. But when she allows the rain to enter her mind, she sees Amy falling off and breaking an arm. Then she falls off. Then the truss drops and lands on all the girls lifting it up. They're all wounded and crying. Miserable. And in last place. They'll never finish the house in time, not it they're all in the infirmary. Then they'll all sleep on the hard ground in tents, in the rain, with their casts to keep them warm.

She sits up. She knows it's early, but she needs answers. Where is Miss Carmine? Flare pulls on some jeans and a sweatshirt. Amy is still asleep and not stirring. Flare tiptoes to the door and grabs her keycard. She doesn't know what she's going out to find, but she can't stay here, listening to time tick away before Mr. Deal's official wakeup call. There's still 45 minutes left.

The faculty stays in another building on the Heaventree campus, Castlebank. It's a medieval looking castle. The other evening when Flare met with Miss Carmine to help gather the girls of the House of Flare, the building seemed like a dream come true. Flare wanted to explore every inch of it. But now, at this time of the morning, in the gray rain, it looks almost scary. Few lights are on inside. Flare pulls her hood over her head to shield her eyes and looks up to the fifth floor where Miss Carmine's room is. It's dark. She's either still asleep or still gone. Flare needs to find out which.

~ 17 ~

The building is locked. Of course, it is. Flare feels the steady pelting of rain on her shoulders and hoodie. She wipes the water from her face. She's got to get in, but how? A light is on to her left. She gets close to the stone building and hides behind the bushes until she's in front of a large window with a small golden light coming from another room.

The window is made up of two vertical panes with metal filigree across the glass. She pushes on the right one but it doesn't budge. She pushes on the left pane and feels the window give beneath the pressure. Her heart stops. She didn't really think she could get the window to open. Now that she's faced with this, she almost has to go in. And isn't this breaking and entering? *Well, I didn't break the window, it just opened*, she tells herself.

She has to be extremely quiet. The window sill is chest level, and the window itself very narrow. Flare hoists herself up on shaking arms, careful not to make a sound. She holds her breath. Her body aches from house building the past couple days. Flare has a surreal moment. She has a hard time comprehending that just four days after she left her parents and home, she's breaking into a castle window.

She lands and hears the drip-dripping of the raindrops off her jacket onto the stone floor. Slowly, she pulls the window shut and tries to take in the room.

It appears to be a small office with a little desk and reading light and shelves of books on one wall. She can only make out silhouettes for the light is emanating from down the hallway. Flare listens hard, but can hear nothing. She peeks out into the hall and heads toward the light. There are large paintings of people on the walls, old men and women, modestly dressed and severe looking. Flare tiptoes across the stone until she comes to the lit room. The door is slightly ajar, and on either side are large stained glass windows showing Biblical scenes of Christ in his ministry. The room is rounded with a cushioned bench along one side, books along the other and a large rose window at the back that will soon cast colored light on the room. Below the rose window is a little table with a small lit lamp. Someone must have left it on, but where is that person now?

Flare pushes the door open and enters the room. This place feels otherworldly, and she has the strong urge to just grab a book and stay here all day. Then she notices the center of the room. There is a round table covered with a tapestry that drapes to the floor and a single ornately carved wooden chair tucked under. On the table rests a large, thick hardcover book. The cover is gilded and dotted with jewels. It appears ancient yet holding up well. Flare moves forward and goes to touch the closed book.

Just as she gets the cover an inch in the air, she hears a noise. Voices.

Flare looks for a place to hide, but there is none! The rounded room has no nooks or crannies. She ducks under the table and prays the tapestry conceals her completely as the voices get closer.

Footsteps. Flare's heart is pounding, and she can barely breathe. Why did she come into this room at all? Why didn't she just go up to the fifth floor and look for Miss Carmine, the whole reason she came here in the first place?!

"...if they find out too soon."

"Yes, have to do everything we can to keep this quiet."

"I don't want to look. You do it."

"All right. But if she's not here, you promise to send someone after her. Promise."

"I do. Let's have a look."

Flare can hear the two people, a man and a woman, standing just beside her. She is sweating and positively knows she'll be found out. The book is opened above her. The heavy cover falls to one side. Pages flip and flip and flip. Finally, they slow.

"Well?"

"Hold on."

"Oh, I knew we shouldn't have sent her."

"She's not here."

"Are you sure? Are you absolutely sure?"

"See for yourself."

It's quiet for a moment, then the woman lets out a deep

sigh. "Then I'll keep my word. I'll send Ashworth after her this morning. But I fear for what he'll find."

The book closes with a thump, and the two scurry out of the room. Flare is left feeling lightheaded. She has no idea what she just heard, but she's sure it has something to do with Miss Carmine. If she's still missing today, she'll be convinced. Flare crawls out on her knees and looks toward the hallway. It's quiet again, but she knows she has to hurry. Mr. Deal's wake up announcement will commence at any time now, and she needs to be back in Chizoba Hall by then.

Flare looks at the huge book again. There are no words on the cover. She lifts it and flips to the first pages. The crisp parchment is stiff in her hands. It has nothing but hand-written names and dates in it. The dates go back thousands of years. Page after page of names. She flips toward the back and finds blank pages. She moves backward now until she comes to the last written page. There are more names. Some have yesterday's date next to them. A couple are dated today. Suddenly, Flare falters. The page she is holding is changing before her very eyes. It's as if a ghost is writing in cursive. Her eyes grow wide. A new name is being written as if from thin air. Flare even hears a scratching noise as if pen to parchment! She drops the page and backs up a step, covering her mouth.

What is this book? What is happening? Letter by letter, the name appears.

Reginald Payne Feinstein   28 August, Year of Our Lord 2116

Then a new name below it:

Sidney Alice Gale Feinstein 28 August, Year of Our Lord 2116
The book is living, breathing. It's continuing to be written! What is this? Magic?

Terrified, Flare shuts the book and runs back over to the door. She makes sure no one is coming, then she retraces her steps to the little office from whence she came. Heart racing, she pushes the window pane open and climbs out, one leg first. She falls to the ground and pulls the window shut, then runs as if her life depends on it. She's got to go find her brother. She has to tell someone what she's seen. She's not altogether sure her mind isn't playing tricks on her, and the only thing that can ground her in reality is seeing Corn's face.

He'll be able to tell her if she's out of her mind or not. Deep down, she knows she saw what she saw, and that what she saw is impossible.

With Christ, all things are possible, she hears in her head. It's her mother's voice. Her mother used to say that to her all the time. Flare ducks into the building just as the rain is beginning to let up. She knows she should be concerned about building the House of Flare today, but this book that writes itself has taken precedence in her thoughts. She'll burst if she doesn't share it soon.

~ 18 ~

There are two huge zebra statues in the entrance of Chizoba Hall, each with a black and white sofa beneath it. Flare runs past them and hears something coming from one of them. Her mind really is playing tricks on her, isn't it?

"Flare," she hears again. It's Amy. She's sitting on the couch to the right. She's already dressed for the day in blue jeans and a pink and green striped shirt. "Where were you?"

"Oh, hey, Amy, I'm sorry, I just...went out."

"In the rain?"

"Yeah, well, I just...hey, what are you doing up already? Has Deal given the wake-up call?"

"Not yet. Could be any minute now. I just woke up and realized you weren't there. I got scared."

Flare walks back to the zebra and sits beneath it, flopping down onto the couch beside Amy. "I'm sorry. You shouldn't be worried about me. I was...just checking on the job site."

"It's wet?"

"It's wet. It'll be a tricky day."

"That's part of why I woke up worrying. I heard the rain. I know we're behind."

"We won't be behind for long." Flare said it, but she's not sure she believes it.

Amy looks at her fingernails. Her pink polish is chipping. "My father was a builder. He slipped one time when it started raining. Broke his leg in three places."

"No kidding," says Flare. "Your father was a builder?"

"Yeah. He used to have his own company before, you know. Before the Global Union. Soon, younger people with chips in their heads could do the work faster. The only jobs he could get were from Christ-followers."

The severity of what she's saying sinks in, and Flare sighs. "Well, I better get back upstairs and get ready. We have a big day ahead of us. Now that I know your father was a builder, I might have to make you the head of our operation. Feinstein Construction Company." As soon as she says it, a chill twists up her spine. "Feinstein," says Flare. "Say, what was your dad's first name?"

"Reggie," says Amy.

"And your mom?"

"Sid."

Reggie and Sid. Reggie and Sid. Reginald and Sidney!

Flare gulps. Her heart pounds. Amy's parents were listed in that book she found, the one that wrote itself! But what does it mean?

In a sprint now, Flare heads for the elevator. She can't wait. She has to find Cornelius and tell him what she knows. The fact that Amy's parents are in that book makes this mystery all the more crucial to solve.

"Good morning, Heaventree!" Flare is in the elevator on her way to Cornelius' floor when Mr. Deal's voice fills the tiny space. "Welcome to day three of our building challenge. For those of you math wizards, this means we have four—count them—four days left to complete our buildings or you and your closest friends will be enjoying the comforts of the ole outdoors. And just look at what she brings you today. It's raining!"

The door opens and Flare steps out onto the hall. The rain falls gently to her side over the railing. Mr. Deal's voice doesn't fade. He's being piped in out here, too. She heads to Cornelius' room.

"I know what you all are waiting for—our rankings," says Deal. "I won't keep you in suspense any longer. The House of Josh has pulled clearly into the lead as all of the trusses are built and the exterior walls have been framed in place. It's actually beginning to look like a structure. Well done, House of Josh. This means that House of Marcus, Houses of Nattie, Atlys, and Cornelius are now neck and neck as trusses are complete but those pesky exterior walls are still not in place. Let's get moving today folks. Houses don't build themselves. And...I guess you all have figured out that House of Flare is still in last place today with one last truss to complete as well as all those walls."

Flare stops and slumps in defeat. She shakes her head and knocks at his door.

"Ladies and gentlemen, I do not need to tell you that the weather will make things tricky today. Safety is of the utmost importance; however time does not slow for anyone. Our Saturday deadline is still very firm. If you require protection from the rain, you will find rain jackets, umbrellas, and tarps in abundance waiting for you. There is also a very nice cluster of oak trees that may provide some relief about a quarter mile away near the lake. Make your plans, stick to them, and now let's go have a big breakfast. You're gonna need it. This is Deal...signing OFF!"

The door opens, and Cornelius stands there dressed with a ball cap and navy windbreaker. The look on his face says it all. His eyes leave hers, and he sniffs and turns around, inviting her to follow. Flare moves past him, hands covering her mouth. He thinks she's upset about being in last place again, but Flare is about to burst with news of the self-writing book.

Joe is in the corner at the sink, brushing his teeth. Flare considers whether or not she should talk in front of Joe. She looks at the clock. There's no time to wait.

"Sis, I'm really sorry, but I think if you can get the last truss built, the rest will go—"

"I know. I'm not worried about that right now."

"You're not? Well, you should be. You're in last place again!"

"What I mean is...listen." She shakes her head, trying to get the jumbled words there to sort in order. "Sit down."

"Okay..." Cornelius pulls out a chair and sits. Joe spits in the sink and wipes his mouth on a towel.

"What I'm about to tell you is, well, strange. Okay. I woke up early, hoping to find Miss Carmine in her room. I went to Castlebank—"

"In the rain?"

"Yes, in the rain. Isn't it obvious?" She smooths her wet hair. "Now listen. I broke into this window and it led me to this room where—"

"You broke into Castlebank?" This time it's Joe piping in. He sits, mesmerized.

"So *listen*." Flare glares at Joe. There's this book there that...well, it has all these names in it, and it writes itself."

"The book writes itself," says Cornelius.

"Yes."

"How do you know?"

"I saw it! I saw the words just appearing out of thin air!"

Cornelius raises his eyebrows, then he takes off his cap, runs his hand over his head and replaces it. "Flare, I know you've been working hard, and you're really stressed. I get that. You miss Mom and Dad, you're in last place—"

Flare slams her hands down on the table in front of him and presses close. Quietly she says, "I know what I saw, Cornelius." She never calls him by his whole name. "I also heard two people talking about the book. I was hiding under this table, and I heard them talking about going and finding someone. I think it was Miss Carmine they were talking about. Corn, I know this sounds crazy, but you have to believe me. Something weird is going on. Books can't write themselves. Miss Carmine has just disappeared. And the weirdest thing of all is that I watched as Amy's parents' names were written into the book. It was like a ghost was writing it. I even heard the scratching on the parchment, but I didn't see anyone there."

"Whoa, whoa," says Cornelius. "You say that Amy's

parent's names were written in it? What kind of book is it?"

"I don't know! It just has name after name after name…and it's old. And huge. It has jewels all over it."

"Cool," says Joe, hanging on her every word.

"Joe, you can't tell anyone about this. Do you understand?" warns Flare.

"No, no, I won't. I won't say a word about the ghosty book."

"Seriously, Joe," says Cornelius. "I believe my sister. She doesn't lie. Well, usually."

"I am not lying, Corn. I promise."

"Okay then, well, we've got a lot to think about today as we're building our houses. In *the rain*."

"Miserable," says Joe. "I don't understand why we have to do this anyway. It's extreme."

"Look, none of us likes it, but it is what it is. Flare, I'd like to talk to Mr. Deal about this—"

"No! Are you kidding? For all I know, he has something to do with Miss Carmine disappearing! How do we know we can trust him? How do we know who we can trust?"

The three are silent, thinking this over.

"Flare, Amy. Does she know?" asks Cornelius.

"Of course not." She stares at her brother and can see something in his eyes. He cares for this girl. It's so obvious.

"Man, I wonder why her parents' names are in there. Maybe it's a roster of some sort. Or an address book. Maybe it has all of our parents' names in it."

"Maybe. I didn't have time to read all of it."

"So let's just get ready for today," says Cornelius,

standing. "I'll at least send Mr. Deal over to help supervise your house if Miss Carmine still isn't there."

"Okay. Thanks," says Flare. She stands and walks to the door, then she turns with her hand on the knob. "Corn?" she asks.

"Yeah?" Cornelius is putting on a brown leather belt.

"You think Mom and Dad are all right? You think they knew what they were getting us into?"

He's quiet as he buckles it. Then he says, "You know, people wake every morning, not knowing what the day brings... But no. I think they probably didn't know what this school was really like. I doubt they knew we'd be building houses. If they did—"

"Maybe they wouldn't have sent us here?" says Flare.

"No. Mom and Dad were dead set on sending us here. There was no question about it. Which makes me think..."

"What?"

"Well, if it's this tough in here at our boarding school, and this was the safer alternative for us, I'm thinking things must be really terrible out in the real world."

This somber thought makes all three of them homesick and presses them toward the door, slightly braver than a moment ago.

~ 19 ~

The rain is coming down in a deluge, washing away dirt mounds and turning them into tiny rivers swirling around Flare and Cornelius' feet. "Three, two, one," they say, and then run as fast as they can from the edge of the building, jackets covering their heads, toward the stash of umbrellas and tarps on the other side of the field. They can't help but laugh. There's something so freeing about running in the rain, feeling the cool water pour over you, soaking you to the bone.

Breakfast was quiet as everyone ate and watched sheets of rain pour down the huge windows. In there they were protected, but out here, nothing shelters the students of Heaventree from the elements.

Shelter.

That's exactly what they need, exactly what they're working toward. No one wants to spend the rest of the school year outside. These houses have to be built.

Cornelius waves to Flare as he runs over to join Joe and the others already waiting in front of the House of Cornelius. His friends look like gnomes under mushrooms, three blue tarps held over their heads.

"The trusses are up," says Cornelius in a voice loud enough to break through the noise of the rain. "Let's tie some tarps on the roof to give us a little shelter!"

The boys go to work, running back and forth for more tarps and rope. Cornelius looks up. It's a long way to the top. He looks at his house mates. He can't ask any of them to do this. It would be too dangerous. It's got to be him. He starts climbing up framed wood walls, careful to place his feet so they don't slip. The muscles in his chest and arms begin to shake when he gets to the top.

"Tie the rope on and throw it up to me!"

The boys hold the tarp while Joe throws the rope up. Over and over, Cornelius misses. It's just too slippery. Evan comes over and reaches on his tiptoes. He's lifting up an umbrella to Cornelius. "Use this!" he calls out.

Cornelius reaches down, careful not to let go or look down. He catches the tip and struggles to bring it up. When the umbrella is opened, he wipes his eyes with the back of his hand and can see again. "One more time!" he calls to Joe. Joe throws up the rope, and this time, it's caught.

After tying the rope in place, Cornelius shimmies up and down the wood until the first tarp is in place, tied off in six places. The 23 boys naturally move under it, and work commences on the next tarps. At this rate, they'll get nothing done except placing tarps. Cornelius is wearing out, yet trying not to act like he's tired.

As he moves up the wood, preparing to tie off another tarp, he stops in his tracks. He hears screaming and sees his sister falling off of her roof.

Heart racing, he looks over to the House of Flare. No, Flare is right there. She's fine. She's climbing up her walls, tying tarps, just as all the heads of houses are, but she's fine.

Huh, thinks Cornelius. *That was weird.* Was it a vision? I dream? He's not sure, but he's got work to do. When he gets the last tarp tied, he climbs down and high-fives his house mates. They're wet, but no longer getting wetter. Celebrating, they pull out a tube and unroll the blueprints for the house. They're getting ready to make a plan for the rest of the day when they all hear screaming. It's over at the House of Flare.

Cornelius already knows in his heart what's happened, and he takes off like a bullet toward his sister.

Flare is lying flat on the ground, her right arm beneath her at an unnatural angle. Her eyes are closed. Cornelius fights the urge to be sick as he holds his sister's left hand shields her face from the rain. "Get a mentor! Quick!"

Quietly, he prays for her.

This can't be happening. She has to be okay. Please! She's all I have left in this world.

Joe and some girls run back with Mr. Deal. He kneels down and looks at her head, opens her eyelids to look at her pupils, then assesses the arm. "Get me a six by two-foot board and some rope!" he hollers. "And a tarp!"

Slowly, Flare, who is still not moving on her own, is lifted carefully and placed on the board. Her red hair is dark and limp, draped over the wood. "Hold her head, Cornelius," says Mr. Deal. "Don't let it move."

"Is her neck broken?" he asks, swallowing.

"Don't know, but not taking any chances. Her arm certainly is."

A group of kids is holding a tarp over Flare, Corn and Mr. Deal. After she's tied on somewhat securely, Amy comes over and puts her hand on Cornelius's shoulder.

"She just fell," she says weakly. "It happened so fast. I'm sorry."

Cornelius nods.

"Okay, on the count of three," says Mr. Deal. He takes a second to wipe the water from his eyes and the black hair glued to his forehead. Then he shakes it back into place. When he grabs the side of the makeshift gurney, Cornelius is frozen in place. He knows he can't have seen what he thinks he just saw. It's not possible.

But he did see it. He's sure if it.

Mr. Deal's forehead.

It had the mark.

~ 20 ~

"Pick it up! Let's go!" shouts Mr. Deal, his eyes intense.

Cornelius lifts his side carefully, and he and Mr. Deal carry an unmoving Flare toward the dining hall as their feet slosh through puddles. Cornelius' mind is reeling. Mr. Deal can't have a mark. He can't be a GUY. Can he? If he is a GUY, what about the others?

Cornelius' confusion gives way to all-out fear, and he wants nothing more than to talk it over with his sister. But she can't talk.

Oh, God, what if she's not okay? What if this is a trick? What if Heaventree isn't what we thought it was at all!

Cornelius hears a moan. It's Flare. Her head rolls over to the side.

"Flare? Flare, can you hear me?!"

"Better not to let her get too awake with that arm," says Mr. Deal. "We'll get her to the infirmary. She'll be all right there."

"Yeah. Okay," says Cornelius.

"You all right?" asks Mr. Deal.

"I guess."

"Let's pray," says Mr. Deal. And he closes his eyes. "Dear heavenly father, we ask for your protection and healing for our sister, Flare. We know she is in your hands, and we trust you. Please give Cornelius a sense of peace as you remove his worry and replace it with trust. Amen."

"Amen," says Cornelius. Maybe he didn't see what he thought he saw. Maybe there's no mark on Mr. Deal's forehead after all. He couldn't pray like that if he was faking it, could he? Could he?

The next two hours are the longest in Cornelius' history, aside from the terrifying ride through the darkness to Heaventree. Joe is in charge of the House of Cornelius today, something that makes Cornelius nervous. With no head for either his or his sister's house, there's no way they won't come in last today. *So be it,* thinks Cornelius. If his sister's house has to stay outdoors all year, he will, too. Right now, all he cares about is making sure his sister is all right.

Flare is lying in a bed in the infirmary. She shares a room with another bed that is empty right now. She's awake and eying the white cast on her right arm. She's quiet, thinking of how stupid it was to fall off the top of the house. She's failing her house mates. What made her ever think she could handle leading a team, anyway?

"Go back to work," says Flare to her brother. "I'm not going anywhere for a while. No use having you get behind on your house too."

"Joe's got it under control. I checked on them a little while ago. The rain is still coming down, but they've built the exterior walls and some on the interior. They're working with the girls in your house, too. If we go down in this, we'll go down together."

"You can't do that," says Flare.

"It's already done. The guys insist on it. I don't even think I'm calling the shots anymore." He smiles and tries to get her to smirk, but she doesn't feel like smiling.

"It'll be okay."

"It won't. My arm is broken in two places."

"So you'll learn to eat with your left hand."

"And hammer? And climb? And...Ugh. Why did this happen? Is anyone else hurt?"

"Not that I know of, but I can't believe there weren't more injuries. This is dangerous stuff we're doing. We're just kids."

"Speak for yourself." At this, Flare smiles and feels more like herself, though her head is fuzzy and the pain is beginning to return to her arm.

"Hey, look at that." Cornelius walks to the window and pulls the curtain aside. "The rain is slowing down. Is it possible?" He looks at his watch. "If it stops raining, we'll have a full six hours to work until it gets dark."

"You better get back out there then."

"I will, but..."

"But what?"

Cornelius moves to the side of her bed and sits down. He leans in and talks barely above a whisper. "I saw something...well, I think I saw something."

"What?" asks Flare.

"It doesn't make sense," he says. "But I thought I saw…" He shakes his head.

"What is it, Corn? We don't have all day. Well, I do, but you don't."

"It's Deal," he whispers. "I think he has…" Cornelius points to his forehead.

"What? And idea? A brain? A head?"

"A mark."

"A wha—no. Can't be."

Cornelius gets up and rubs the back of his neck.

"Corn," says Flare, "that's crazy. If that's true, think about it. That changes everything. Everything we think about this place—"

"I know. Would be a lie."

"There you are," says Mr. Deal, entering the doorway while knocking on the frame. "How is our patient?"

Cornelius jolts and moves in front of Flare instinctively. "She's fine. Better. She will be anyway."

"Good. Good. I'm sorry about your arm. That's unfortunate."

"Thank you for bringing me in here," says Flare.

"Just doing my job," he says. "I'm no hero. You're brother, on the other hand…"

"We always look out for each other," says Cornelius, forcefully.

"I should hope so," says Mr. Deal. "I especially like how your housemates are helping out the House of Flare. When one of us is down, we're all down. Right? So Flare, get back on your feet. You'll need to do more delegating from the wings. Doesn't look like you'll be lifting a hammer this week."

"But have you heard anything about Miss Carmine?" she asks.

"Miss Carmine...no. I'm afraid I have not."

"How could she just leave us? She was my mentor, right? It doesn't make sense."

Mr. Deal looks at Flare a little longer than normal, then shakes his head. "I'm sure she has a good reason, wherever she is. Now, what you must do is the best you can do. You'll be surprised at the progress they're starting to make out there. All of your trusses are completed, and if this rain clears, you might even have a part of a roof today. After that, it's all downhill." He looks at her cast. "Well, you know what I mean. Keep your chin up."

"I will," says Flare.

"Cornelius, how about I escort you back to work? Your housemates could use another two hands."

Flare catches Cornelius' eye as he turns on the way out. It's impossible. She can't believe Mr. Deal is a GUY. He's too nice. He can't be faking his love for Christ. The prospect is too scary. Then she remembers her missing mentor and the book that writes itself.

Perhaps nothing is impossible in Heaventree. What do they really know about this place, anyway?

Flare puts her left hand on her hard cast and closes her eyes to ward off the pain. Then she sits up slowly. She won't be staying in here any longer. She's got to get back out there and somehow get back in the game. There's too much to do, and now, too many questions to answer.

$$\sim 21 \sim$$

"And just where do you think you're going?"

Flare stops in her tracks. It's not a nurse or doctor; it's Remley, the maintenance man.

"Oh, hi. I, uh, I need to get back to work."

Remley smiles and leans on his broom. "You took quite a fall." He looks in the hallway to a chart on the wall. "This, here, says you're s'posed to stay overnight for observation."

"Hmm. Really? Well, I'm feeling fine."

"Maybe, but the doctor knows what he's talking about. Why don't you just get on back in that bed?"

Flare turns and looks out the window. It's stopped raining. "I'll rest later."

"I see." Remley begins sweeping outside the room and moves out of eyeshot. Finally, he peeks his head back around the corner and whispers. "If'n you were to stay here overnight, I have it on good authority that there might just be something you want to see."

"Like what?" asks Flare.

"Can't say. What I will say is you'd have to be mighty

quiet if'n you were to sneak around in a place like this in the dark."

The hairs on the back of Flare's neck tingle. What is he saying to her? What is it that she needs to stay and see? And why is Remley telling her any of this? Before she has a chance to ask him, he's darted back out the doorway. She goes to look for him, but he's gone. Only the nurse's station at the end of the hall is busy. The rest of the place? Completely dead.

Nightfall comes on slowly. Too slowly. For Flare, it's been the longest day of her life. She's dying to know what's going on with her housemates. She puts her pudding spoon back in the bowl and closes her eyes. Her medication is making her sleepy.

She hears a knock and startles.

"You taking visitors?" says a voice. It's a nice voice. Attached to a nice body.

"Josh," says Flare, trying to sit up straighter. What does her hair look like? She runs her right hand through it and wipes her mouth.

"Yep, it's me, and Nattie, and Marcus. Cornelius is coming in a bit. He's still out there working with a flashlight."

"Corn," says Flare, smiling, thinking about her brother. Nattie comes in and leans down to hug her.

"Does it hurt much?" asks Nattie.

"Nah. Throbs a little."

"We all pitched in and got your house caught up," she says. "You're in the lead."

"No," says Flare. "No, you guys, you shouldn't have done that!"

Marcus pulls the marker off of Flare's chart on the wall in the hallway and comes closer. "You would do the same for one of us. Yes?"

"Yes, I guess," she says.

"Good. Then you understand. We all know what it's like to lead a house. It's not easy." He sits on the edge of the bed and pulls off the marker cap. "May I?" he asks, hovering over the cast.

Flare smiles. Marcus signs his name on her cast, and then Josh and Nattie follow suit. This feeling of comradery is not anything she's felt at Heaventree until now. "Where's Atlys?" she asks.

Everyone's quiet for a second. Then Nattie says, "Atlys has other ideas about getting ahead this week. She...she and her house opted not to help."

"Oh. Well, maybe they had too much going on."

"We all did. And we all managed."

"Yeah, but the prospect of sleeping out in that rain will make you do funny things," says Flare, blowing it off.

"I guess so," says Nattie.

"But you guys. I can't thank you enough. I hope to return the favor someday. I know all the girls in my house appreciate it."

Josh stands at the foot of the bed. Looking at him, having him this close, makes Flare feel flushed. What is wrong with her? He crosses his arms, and his muscles bulge. "We decided we're going to beat Heaventree at its own game," he says. "If we all work together, nobody loses."

"What if we all lose? What if we all don't make it?"

"There's a chance, but it's small," says Josh. "Anyway,

too late now. It's a plan. It's official. Look, we're going to get out of here and let you get your rest. I'm really glad you're okay. We were worried."

"See you tomorrow?" asks Nattie.

"Definitely," says Flare. "And thank you. Again."

After her friends leave, Flare is left smiling. Part of her thinks breaking her arm was the best thing that could have happened to the House of Flare. If she hadn't, they'd probably still be out there, struggling in last place!

She's still smiling when Cornelius and Amy come in. They're both filthy.

"Hard day?" she asks.

"Not as hard as yours," says Amy. "Everybody came together out there. Our house is looking amazing."

"Amy's already picking out wallpaper," teases Cornelius. She nudges him with her elbow and Flare raises and eyebrow. It's apparent these two are becoming quite comfortable with each other.

"No, really," says Cornelius. "You'd be proud of Amy. She stepped up today as a real leader. She even yelled."

"I did not yell."

"You yelled at me!"

"That's because you were goofing around and about to get hurt!"

"You two look like wet rats," says Flare. "You ought to clean up and go to bed. I'm afraid I won't be that much help tomorrow either."

"Oh, I almost forgot," says Amy. "I brought you some fresh clothes and your toothbrush." She hands her a backpack.

"Heaven," says Flare.

"Amy, give me just a minute, would you?" asks Cornelius. Amy heads out the door, and Cornelius scoots in close and sits on the bed.

"Something's going on here," says Flare when she's sure Amy's out of earshot. "I'm going to poke around a little bit."

"You can't."

"I can, and I will. I have to."

"Uggh. You're impossible. Just be careful and don't get caught," says Cornelius. "I'm still convinced Mr. Deal had a mark. I don't want to believe it, but I know what I saw."

"And I believe you. If Deal's an imposter, then we're all in trouble and have a whole lot more to worry about than sleeping in the rain."

"I wish I could stay. Maybe I can stay here tonight," says Cornelius.

"I'll be out in the morning and everything will be fine. You're needed back at Chizoba Hall. You know...for Joe and your housemates. And Amy."

Flare watches for pink on her brother's cheeks, and he doesn't disappoint. "Come here, kid." She holds her one good arm out, and Cornelius leans in for a hug. "I'm really proud of you, you know. Whatever happens, I'm...well, I'll see you tomorrow. Just get outta here."

When Cornelius is gone, Flare sits up straighter. She's exhausted, but she can't succumb to the painkillers. Not now. Remembering Remley's conversation about some secret she needed to see tonight, Flare rubs her eyes. She's got to stay alert long enough to sneak around the infirmary. How she'll do it without getting caught, she has no idea. But she has to try.

~ 22 ~

In the still darkness of her room, Flare awakes, eyes opening slowly. Her arm hurts, and it all comes back to her—she's in the infirmary. She remembers the fall in the rain. She remembers her brother's face. She remembers Remley leaning on his broom. She bites her lip, fully awake now, alert. She hears sounds down the hallway, footsteps, beeps. There is light coming from under her door.

Flare's heart begins to race. What time is it? Stars shine in the blackness of night outside her window. Sitting up, she acclimates herself. She has to be quiet, and it's not going to be easy with this cast. She feels with her left hand and makes sure the way is clear as she slides off the bed. She feels her body to see what she's wearing. The same clothes—shorts and a t-shirt, and socks. No need for shoes. Maybe she'll be quieter that way.

Flare breathes in deeply and exhales. *Lord, please let me find what you want me to see. Please don't let me get caught either. Protect me and be my refuge. Thank you for never leaving me. Amen.*

It's now or never. Flare tiptoes over to the door and turns the knob slowly. She pads her way down the hall, close to the wall, away from the nurses' station. At the end of the hall, she finds a stairwell marked Emergency Exit. Will an alarm go off if she pushes the door?! She decides she has to take the chance. *One, two, three!* She pushes and...no alarm sounds.

In the stairwell, she sees she's on the fourth floor. Up or down? She decides to head up. Step by step, she prays for guidance. How do you go searching for something when you have no idea what you're looking for? Where do you go? She just keeps climbing. Finally, she's on the top floor. The seventh. She pulls the door open and sees a darkened hallway. The only light is the bit of moonlight coming in from the windows of the open rooms. Perhaps this hall is not in use.

Flare trains her eyes and walks carefully in the dim light. When she gets to the empty nurses' station, she hears something. Voices.

Flare follows the murmur until the voices become clearer. There is a light on down at the end of one of the four hallways. The infirmary seems to be laid out in the shape of a cross. Flare leans against the wall and hides in the shadows. She inches closer until she can hide herself in a doorway and peek around to watch what's going on. People move in the room quickly and shuffle out.

"Give her some space..."

"...need to increase her meds..."

"Can you hear me?"

There is a sound coming from the room, a machine beeping at a consistent pace.

Flare feels her heart beating in time with the machine.

She closes her eyes, presses against the doorway, and tries to calm down. She's not sure how long she's been standing here, but it seems like forever. Finally, there are no more voices, only the beeping. Is everyone gone? Flare needs to know who's in that room. Why would there be some lone person on this floor when no one else is up here?

She leans out the door and makes her way on socked feet to the room. Slowly, slowly, being careful not to make a noise and careful to listen for any movement. When she finally stands at the doorway, she sees a sad sight—a person in the bed, hooked up to machines. There are bandages covering the head and most of the body showing outside the thin white sheet. The machine monitors the heart rate.

Holding her breath, Flare looks around the room for clues as to who it could be. Then she stops and grabs at her throat. It feels like it's closing. There's a necklace sitting on the little table beside the bed. She feels her own necklace. She picks it up to her lips and pushes the button. She whispers, "Miss Carmine?"

Flare hears the echo of her own voice around her. She sees a shock of purple hair sticking out of the back of the bandages.

It's Miss Carmine! She's here and terribly hurt! Tears threaten Flare's eyes as she steps closer. So that's why she disappeared. She's in here! Who did this to her?

Flare moves in closer and looks behind her to be sure no one is coming. She gets right next to the body and grabs the two fingers that aren't bandaged. It's Miss Carmine, all right. Her fingernails are painted lavender and chipped. "Miss Carmine, it's me, Flare," she whispers. "I'm so glad to find you. I'm so sorry you're hurt. Who did this to you?"

She doesn't receive an answer. Flare swallows. She can do nothing for her, but she's dying to know what happened. Something terrible is going on. Did this happen at Heaventree? Will it happen to Flare and the others?

Quickly and quietly, Flare leaves the room and heads back down the darkened hallway. She's got to get back to her room before anyone finds her missing. Her mind is spinning—relieved to see that Miss Carmine is here, alive, thank God, and that she didn't leave her for no good reason, but terrified at the same time. She's got to get out of here and warn the others. Whatever happened to Miss Carmine could happen to them. The thought of Corn in trouble makes her quicken her pace.

~ 23 ~

Cornelius and Joe stumble into the Main Hall for breakfast. Literally. They're so hungry, they keep pushing the other one out of the way so they can get to the buffet first. The room is already filled with the clanking of dishes and quiet hum of conversations. Cornelius piles bacon on top of buttered grits and grabs two biscuits.

"Eggs?" asks a woman replacing an empty platter with one overflowing with them.

"Mmm." He nods and adds a pile of scrambled eggs to his plate. Joes grabs the spoon after him.

When they're seated at a long table with Evan and the rest of the House of Cornelius, Joe says, "I don't think I can keep up like this. I'm so hungry I could eat my fist. Your fist, even."

Corn would say something, but he can't. His mouth is too full.

"I didn't realize how hard this would be," said Evan. "This is nothing like building that birdhouse with my dad." He looks sad. Cornelius feels the need to step in. He knows how it feels to miss his parents. He's missing them right this very minute.

"This is just like camp, guys. We'll have our house built in a few days, then we'll move in—"

"Where are we all going to sleep?" asks Joe.

"I'm sure we'll have beds and all that. Don't worry about what comes next. We have to stay focused on what we're doing today."

"Focus on our daily bread?" says Evan.

"Exactly. Only our daily bread." He picks up his biscuit and breaks it in half. "We don't need to worry about anything else."

"Guys!" Flare is limping toward her brother with her cast out in front of her.

"What are you doing here?" says Cornelius. "I was going to come check on you. How did you get out so—"

"Never mind. You gotta listen to this. You won't believe what I saw."

Cornelius notices the uneasy look in her eye as she realizes Joe and Evan and the rest of the boys are watching her, listening.

"Guys, give me a minute," says Cornelius, standing and moving toward Flare after shoving half the biscuit in his mouth.

They walk outside to the picnic tables by the lake. Flare can't help but remember sitting here talking with Miss Carmine the first day they arrived at Heaventree. She was so young, so pretty, and now...

"It's Miss Carmine," says Flare, sitting on the bench and watching a swan on the lake. "I saw her. She's in the infirmary. She's in really, really bad shape."

"Like what? What happened to her?"

"I have no idea."

"You didn't ask her?"

"She couldn't talk!" says Flare. "I mean, she's covered from head to toe in bandages. Her face was even covered up."

Cornelius is quiet for a moment. He pushes the hair off his forehead. "I hate to be so obvious, but Flare, how do you know it was her if her face was covered?"

Flare picks up her necklace and shows it to Cornelius. "Remember she gave me this? Her matching necklace was on the table next to her. And I saw her purple hair. And her purple nails. It was her, I know it."

"There you are!" It's Professor Moss, waggling her finger. "You had us worried sick!" Atlys comes alongside her, looking down as if studying the concrete. "Why are you here and not in the infirmary, young lady? The whole place is in an uproar. Imagine. Losing a student."

"I—I feel okay. I just wanted to get back with my house."

"Did it ever occur to you that there is proper protocol to go through? One cannot simply walk out of the infirmary without checking out and letting adults know you are leaving! Not to mention, your doctors haven't given you the freedom to leave. Come with me now." She holds her swollen-fingered hand out to Flare, who doesn't budge, only looks at her brother for help.

"Professor Moss," he says, standing, "I'm sure there's a misunderstanding. My sister is fine to supervise her house this morning, I'm sure of it, but I will personally escort her back to the infirmary just to get her doctor's okay."

"Well, no, I will take her there—"

"And leave the House of Atlys with no mentor? From what I heard, your house has risen in the ranks. At this rate, it may be coming in first place."

Atlys seems to perk up and almost grin. Professor Moss looks at her and puts a hand on her shoulder, taking pride in anything good her student is doing. Not to mention it appears to dawn on her that with Cornelius taking her back to the infirmary, both he and Flare, two heads of houses, will be MIA, something that will certainly help her precious Atlys to succeed.

"Well, I—if you'll promise to hurry along and not dawdle."

"Yes, Ma'am," says Cornelius.

"It was ir-re-sponsible," says Professor Moss, pointing a finger at Flare again.

"Yes, Ma'am," says Flare.

The short log of a woman huffs and turns. She and Atlys start on their way when Cornelius stops them. "Professor Moss, I forgot to ask you. How did you know Flare was gone?"

"Why, when we went to visit her, of course. We were very, very worried about her."

"I see. Well, we all went by last night after our work was done. Atlys, you didn't come with us. And strangely, yours was the only house not to pitch in and help the House of Flare, even though you knew she was hurt and of course, you were very, very worried about her."

Atlys opens her mouth, but nothing comes out but "I—"

"We don't have time for this immaturity, Mister

Flanagan. There is much work to do, and we've no time to waste on your...well, quite frankly, your un-Christian-like tone."

With that, she barrels away with her blonde protégé in tow as Flare and Cornelius watch, stunned.

"What in the world was all of that?" asks Flare.

"I told you. It wasn't pretty yesterday. Everybody came together except them. And she's calling me un-Christian."

"She doesn't know what she's talking about. Corn, I don't want to go back to the infirmary. I'm afraid they won't let me go."

"No, I don't think they will. And we've only got three days to finish our houses."

"So you won't take me back? But you promised Professor Moss."

"I did...but she already told me what she thinks of me. Why change her mind now?" Smiling, he puts an arm around his sister. "Not to mention, something in my spirit tells me there's no time to waste. Something's going on here... first that magic book you saw and now Miss Carmine getting hurt. Come on, it's going to take you a while to get to the building site in your shape. We better start now."

If it weren't for her wishing she could be out there, helping, Flare might enjoy this. Nailing, hammering—it's almost as if an orchestra is sounding, the players all over the place. The Houses of Flare, Cornelius, Marcus, Josh, Nattie, and Atlys are finally taking shape. Six houses all in a row. They have roofs, walls, window and door openings.

Now it's all about finishing up. The plumbing and electrical is next. Then floors, siding, sheetrock, window and door installation.

Come to think of it, Flare is not enjoying this. There's too much to do and too little time! Propped in a chair on the dirt, she awkwardly rolls the blueprints back up and holds them on her legs. She watches Amy struggling to haul a load of pipes and fittings to the girls inside the house. Well, it doesn't really look like a house. More like a barn. Great, they're all going to be living like animals in barns. But, cool barns they built with their own hands, Flare reminds herself. Yes, pretty cool they've done this on their own.

After twenty minutes, she's had enough. Flare can't sit here, watching. She has to be in the middle of it all. She uses her good arm to carry her folding chair into the House of Flare. She sits there in the middle, admiring the roof, the framing. All of it is magnificent. She is overwhelmed with gratitude and pride for the girls in her house. Amy and Kastia are working on plumbing. Selena and Regan are nailing up plywood. Through the side doorway, Flare sees the boys at the House of Cornelius next door. How have they come so far in less than a week? She wonders. How is it possible it's only been days since she and her brother left their parents? How are they doing? She wonders. Her heart aches, and tears come to her eyes. She can't wait to tell them all about their experiences here. She can't wait to tell her mom and dad how proud she is of her little brother, of the young man he is becoming.

Then the memory of Miss Carmine grips her. She grabs

her necklace and puts the pendant to her lips. Even if she tries to call her, Miss Carmine won't answer. Can't answer. And people are probably in her room with her. She hesitates, closes her eyes, and then holds down the little button and whispers, "Miss Carmine...are you there? It's me."

She takes her thumb off and hears nothing but static.

If she's honest, sometimes it's how she feels when she talks to God. She calls out but hears nothing back but static. Even though she knows He's there.

That's where faith comes in, she can almost hear her father say. His faith always seems unshakable. *Oh, Dad, what's going on back home? How are you and Mom?*

Flare's eyes fill with tears, and this time, they spill over.

~ 24 ~

Friday morning. Only two days left to build the houses. Only TWO days! Cornelius has been up for an hour, staring at the blueprint, trying to figure out how to get it all done. It seems impossible.

And then it gets worse.

"Good morning, fine sirs and ladies," calls Mr. Deal from the loudspeakers. "It is time to rise and shine and face a new day the Lord has given us. On that note, let us start with a Scripture. 'Day after day, in the temple courts and from house to house, they never stopped teaching and proclaiming the good news that Jesus is the messiah.' Good news indeed. This from the book of Acts. Let us remember, friends, to never stop proclaiming the good news we have in Jesus, our loving Savior.

"And now, for the not-so-good-news. As you know, each of you has been working very hard this week and is to be commended. However. Due to circumstances beyond our control...you will all have only one more day to finish your house."

"What?!" Cornelius cries.

"Are you kidding?!" yells Joe.

"No exceptions," says Mr. Deal. "One more day. Today, in fact. By sundown, your houses must be complete or you will be sleeping...well, you know. In the beginning, when God created the heavens and the earth, He did so in six days and on the seventh rested. And so you shall complete your work in six days. Do not ask questions, do not grumble amongst yourselves or you will only waste time. That being said, go now to breakfast and make no haste. Go. Now. Good day."

Joe and Cornelius stare at each other in the deafening silence, their eyes wide. Cornelius' heart is pounding. He stands up and throws some sweatpants on and a ball cap. Joe does the same. This isn't happening. It can't be. There's no way they can finish today. ONE day.

Is the administration of Heaventree demented? Cruel? Is this some kind of joke? Without a word, Cornelius and Joe run out of the room and head for the Main Hall. Mr. Deal said no questions, but Cornelius has to know what's going on. He's going to track down Mr. Deal and get to the bottom of this. It's just not fair to any of them. Suddenly, being the leader of the House of Cornelius just got a whole lot less fun.

He finds him having a cup of coffee on the back veranda of the Main Hall. He's at the picnic tables by himself, staring off over the lake.

"Mr. Deal," says Cornelius.

Mr. Deal turns and looks at him warily. Then barely, he smiles. "I figured I'd see you soon."

"Sir..." Cornelius comes closer and cautiously forms his words. He breathes in deeply. "I know you said no questions, but I really have to ask what's going on here. With all due respect, we cannot possibly complete every last detail on these houses by sundown. Maybe one or two houses will come close, but...sir, I don't think it's fair. Are you really going to have people sleeping outdoors? And will we be able to continue working on these houses to finish them or are we all going to live in open-air barns with no electricity or plumbing? It doesn't make sense."

Mr. Deal sips his coffee again. He pulls his ball cap down further on his forehead. Then he seems to notice Cornelius's eyes staring where the mark would be.

Cornelius looks down quickly. *He knows that I know.*

"I knew I liked you from the moment you stepped out on the stage, Mr. Flanagan. You are smart, but more than that, courageous. I was very clear about not asking questions, was I not?"

"Yes, sir, but—"

"You feel you are above the rules?"

"Not at all. I just...I need to stand up and speak when something isn't right. It's how I was raised."

"Yes. How you were raised." He walks away a few steps and sits down on top of a picnic table. "Come. Sit down."

Cornelius sits a level lower on the seat next to his mentor.

"Tell me about your parents."

"Sir? I don't think this has any—"

"Please. Tell me."

"Well, they're great," says Cornelius. "They're loving and taught us everything. They love God with all their hearts and raised us to do the same. It hasn't been easy for them. Or us, I guess. It's not easy having to hide your true identity, being a person of faith, not having a..." He swallows. Should he say it? He feels like he can trust Mr. Deal when he's talking to him like this, but Cornelius knows what he saw. He saw the mark on his forehead. He may be speaking with the enemy right now. Cornelius stops talking and looks at his feet.

"You know, don't you," says Mr. Deal. Cornelius doesn't move. "Look at me."

Cornelius turns slowly and watches Mr. Deal reach up and pull his cap off. His mouth falls open. There's no chip there, only a nasty, deep scar. "Sir, what happened?"

"I didn't grow up like you did, Cornelius. In my house, I was the firstborn. I got my chip when I was a child. I had no choice. My parents implanted me on my second birthday. The G.O.D. chip responds to your age. It gives a toddler the information he needs. It changes as you get older, downloading more and more until you are a perfected Global Citizen. You are flooded with knowledge and have no time for thoughts of your own. No room for imagination or rebellion."

"So how did you...what happened?"

Mr. Deal sighs heavily. "There are some who are exceptions to the rule, some who, even though they are flooded night and day with information, have room in their minds to think. It's a partitioning, if you will. I was able to set aside the chatter and to imagine, to think on my own, though it was not easy." He stands up and walks to the water's edge. Cornelius follows.

"I learned how to work around the system. I learned

how to navigate and access new libraries of information, ones that weren't being fed to us. I learned to feed myself."

"All with your head?"

"All with my head and the chip, yes."

"Wow."

Mr. Deal turns and looks at Cornelius. His face reddens. His scar turns whiter. His voice gets softer. "One day, I accessed a hidden file. In it was information about every religion that ever existed and all of world history. This was stuff no one knew about. My mind was, well...when you learn something from the chip, you download everything at once. You get an understanding of the entire topic all at the same time. Cornelius, when it came to Christianity, the entire Bible was downloaded into my head. I had all the Scriptures, everything, all at once. And I'm telling you, it was as if everything else I had ever learned made deeper sense in an instant. There is power in God's Word, as you know, and this power...freed me. I could see my miserable state. I could see the state of my world. I understood who we were as humans and how we were being made into machines with no souls. I understood evil in an instant. And I understood Good.

"After a while, it became unbearable. So when I was about your age, I removed my chip."

"How?"

"You don't want to know. But you cannot understand what silence sounds like when you've had nothing but chatter in your brain all your life. I could think. I could question. I could imagine. And that's when I heard God's voice in my spirit. It was like nothing I had ever heard before. A beauty I can't describe."

"I know his voice," says Cornelius. "Trust me. I know."

Mr. Deal wipes his eyes and puts his cap back on. "When the chip was removed, I didn't lose the information that had already been downloaded. I know thousands of texts and books and history. And I know word for word the Scriptures. I began to see my place in history, began to understand the prophecies. I knew what was coming, and so I started planning for this school."

"Wait. You're the one? My dad said in his letter that there was a man he was told about in his visions, someone who was starting this school. It was you?'

"'Fraid so."

"Well, what does this school have to do with the prophecies?"

"As we've already talked about, the end is coming. Jesus will return someday. But before that, things are going to get bad. Very bad."

"Are you saying that's going to happen soon?"

"Cornelius. You only need to know what you need to know. Nothing more."

"You have to tell me. Sir. Please."

"You need to get back and finish your house, Cornelius. All of you do."

"Is this why we only have one more day? Does this have something to do with it? Please, you have to be honest with me now."

Mr. Deal inhales sharply. "Mr. Flanagan, if I tell you

something now, will you promise—and I mean not one word—promise not to say anything to anyone, including your sister."

Cornelius is frozen. He needs to know. But not tell Flare? He makes his decision. "I promise, sir."

"Very well. I'm going to tell everyone this tomorrow, but not until then. It's too devastating and no one will be able to focus on their work. Are you sure you want to know?"

"No sir. But I have to now."

Mr. Deal places his hand on Cornelius' shoulder and looks into his eyes. "The world, as we know it, as you knew it, is ending. As we speak. Everything outside the walls of Heaventree is falling to destruction. There's a new directive from the G.O.D. satellite being fed into the chips of G.U.Y.s all over the world. There are orders to kill anyone without a chip."

"What do you mean? Kill? Really? My parents?"

Mr. Deal nods. "I'm afraid so. Every person of faith is in danger, anyone without the chip...unless they've gone into hiding like we have—"

Cornelius feels weak in the knees. He needs to go tell Flare. Needs to see her. Needs to hug her. Needs to see his parents!

"Cornelius, I need you to be strong. I can't sugarcoat this at all. I wish I could. But understand this. The houses you are building are for a reason. We will need them soon. Do you understand? We will need those houses so you must complete them as best you can. Because to-morrow...tomorrow we tell all you kids the truth. Son, this is their last day of innocence. Don't take that from them. Do you hear me?"

Cornelius grabs onto Mr. Deal's arm and squeezes. He feels like he might implode. He squeezes and gasps for air, tears slipping down his face. And then...he wipes his eyes. He stares into those of his mentor and gathers himself. He thinks of saying thank you, sir, for telling him the truth, but can't find it in himself to thank him for this. His parents may be dead right now. All of their parents may be dead. Cornelius has to hold this in for a day. He can't tell a soul. He wishes he didn't know himself.

Without another word, Cornelius turns and walks away from Mr. Deal and closer to the Houses. Somehow he's got rejoin the innocent, inspire them to keep working and finish what they started.

All this.

All today.

All while the world is ending.

~ 25 ~

When the sun is high in the sky, Flare steps outside her house to take a sip of water. She sees Josh walking toward her. She swallows wrong and coughs. "You all right?" he asks.

"Great. Yeah," she says, wiping her mouth on the back of her hand.

"Good. Whoa. Is this...where's your door? And windows?"

"Ugg. Is it that obvious?" Flare turns around and walks inside. Josh follows. The girls look up at him for a second and then get back to work. "If I could use my other arm, I'd be a lot more help around here."

"Well, let me help. Here, I can pick up a window. Look. Just help me get this in place."

Josh hoists the window up over his knees and walks it in place. Flare's not too proud to accept this offer. There's simply no time to be proud. She helps him push it into the opening in the wall. "It fits!" she says. "Here, let's go do another one." Window after window, she follows Josh around, helping to push the windows in place. She'll get someone to help her with nails and caulk after he leaves.

Wait a minute, she thinks. Josh has his own house to handle.

"I really don't know how to thank you, but you've got to get back to your house. Please. We've got this from here."

"Are you sure?" he asks. "I mean, I hate to tell you, but you may still be—"

"In last place. I know."

"Well, look. If your house comes in last, I'll pitch my tent right next to yours."

"Come on." Flare feels like she's blushing. She wishes she could hide her face.

"I'm serious, Flare. We all will. If they make one house sleep outside, then we'll beat the system and refuse to sleep inside our houses."

"That's seriously sweet but totally stupid, Josh. It doesn't hurt Heaventree at all if we sleep outdoors."

"Maybe. Maybe not. But they might just see we're serious about sticking together and have a change of heart."

Flare's the one with the change of heart. What in the world is happening? A week ago, when she first arrived at Heaventree, she thought Josh was obnoxious. Now, she's not sure. Is it possible he's even better looking now? Is it his sweaty hair? The dirt on his face? What? She has to look away.

"Thank you for the windows," she says to her shoes. "Now get out of here before I come over to your house and slow things down with this stupid cast."

Josh stares at her for a moment until she looks up at him again. She catches him smiling. Flare smiles too, weak-kneed, then turns around and shuts her imaginary door in his face.

After a quick sandwich, Flare assesses her house. She's impressed. It has windows and doors, a roof and walls. It may not be painted or pretty, so far from her original daydreams of columns and décor, but it's shelter. "Ladies, come take a quick seat," she calls. The hammering stops and slowly, they dribble in. The girls, all 23 of them, stare at her from the floor and lean against walls. Amy is in the corner, wiping sawdust off her forehead.

"All right, House, I just wanted to take one minute to tell you how proud I am of you. Of all of us. I have never seen anybody work as hard as we have in the past six days. Ever. We went from not knowing how to hammer, to building this entire structure by hand. Look at it! I am blown away and, well, really honored to be your friend." Flare tears up, and it catches her off guard. She's not the crying type.

"Anyway, I know this is the last day. We've only got about eight more hours. You've done a really good job of not complaining. It's totally unfair of them to change the rules on us and take away a day, and you've just rolled with it. So...I want us to keep working and maybe tomorrow we'll get that day of rest." She studies her cast and runs her fingers over it. "I also want to say how sorry I am for getting hurt."

"It's not your fault," says Amy.

"But we're down one arm and half a person. I truly am sorry for that. I just hope we don't come in—"

"How about we get back to work, then, boss?" says

Marley, the freckled girl who challenged her a week ago. "We've got a house to finish." Smirking, Marley stands and the rest of them follow and head back to their tasks.

Flare takes a second to enjoy the feelings she has for these girls, then decides it's time to check on her brother's house. It's strange. She hasn't seen him all day.

Cornelius feels like he might throw up. He's sweating, nailing siding to the outside of his house, avoiding all the guys. He feels like being alone. His mind is racing with worry. There's a war going on outside Heaventree. His parents are out there. They're targets. Where will they go? Why didn't they come to Heaventree with Flare and him? Did Dad have a plan? Have they gone into hiding? And what about the others? He bites his lip and hurls another piece of siding up. He's bound to get this thing finished. He doesn't know what it's for, what all of this is for, but he trusts Mr. Deal now. At least he feels better about that.

"Hey, Corn," says Flare.

"Ahh!" Cornelius screams and drops his board.

"Whoa, sorry."

"Don't sneak up on people like that," he snips.

"You were hammering. I—wow, this place is looking really good. I'm impressed."

"Yeah. Well, the guys are working hard."

"You okay? You don't look good," says Flare. "Maybe you need to rest a minute."

"I can't rest. There's too much to do."

"Okay, okay, I get it, but...you sure you're all right? You look worried. I don't think you're going to come in last. It's going to be my house, so no biggie."

Cornelius sighs and looks at his sister. She thinks the worst thing that will happen is that the girls in the House of Flare will have to sleep in tents. She has no idea how bad things are. She has no idea Mom and Dad...

Cornelius swallows and turns away from her. He doesn't want her to see in his eyes that he knows more. She'll get it out of him. She always does. He's never been able to keep a secret well. He's so raw, so close. He picks up a board and starts hammering again. "You better get back to work!" he yells over the noise. "Love you, sis."

"Okay...I guess. See you later."

Flare walks away slowly. *Please go away*, thinks Cornelius. *Don't turn around. Don't ask any more questions. Just go.*

So she does. And Cornelius fights back tears as he hammers, and hammers, and hammers at his worst fear. *Are our parents dead?*

~ 26 ~

A whistle is blown. Mr. Deal yells through a megaphone, "Everyone, hammers down. Our day is done. Most of you have electricity, so you could continue to work inside, but I must ask you to stop now. Put everything down, just as it is."

The sound of hammering and movement stops.

"A late dinner, no, *feast*, has been prepared for you," he says. "Come. Let us celebrate the work of our hands and the work of our God together. You have five minutes."

Mr. Deal sounds tired. Everyone is tired. Flare can't believe how hard they've worked over the past six days, and especially today. From the outside, all of the houses, well, *barns* look finished. It's amazing to see the row of them that wasn't there just days ago. So much has happened. Flare's made friends. She's built with her hands. Left home. Grown up some. With quiet resignation she puts her good arm around Amy and smiles weakly to the rest of the girls to follow her. It's a slow, sad procession to the dining hall. The truth lies behind them. Flare turns around and sees the row of six houses from afar. The House of Flare is the only one without lights. They just didn't have time to finish the electrical work.

That's it. They lost. Time to go face the judge.

It's a solemn affair. The dining hall hums with a low murmur, nothing like the excited voices they expected to have when their work was complete. Although famished, the students line up patiently to wash their hands in the restrooms first.

Flare washes her left hand and sees herself in the mirror. She looks different. Same red hair. A cast on her arm, yes, but it's more than that. She studies her eyes. They know more. Have seen more. She likes what she sees just a little more, even though she's dusty and sweaty and tired-looking. It's the inside she's more comfortable with. She and her friends know they did their best. It may not be fair, but they came in last. Tent City, here they come.

"Fearing something is sometimes worse than the real thing," she says to her reflection.

"What's that?" asks Marley, turning off the faucet beside her and grabbing for a towel.

"Oh, nothing. I was just thinking how much I worried all week about us losing. About us having to sleep in tents. And now...well, now it's here, we lost and...somehow, I'm not as afraid anymore. I'm just really sorry I let you guys down."

"You didn't let us down. We just aren't the fastest builders. That's all."

"Yeah, well."

Marley leans over and gives Flare a conciliatory hug. She catches their image in the mirror, and time seems to stand still for a second. She and Marley have become friends this week. That's worth something.

Flare hears music. Singing. *Time to go face the music,* she thinks. She and Marley head to their table but stop as soon as they enter the dining hall. Everyone is standing in place, singing, some with hands raised, some with swaying hands, some holding hands. A wooden cross is propped up in front of the mentor's table, in front of the stained glass. She's not sure who started it, but a chorus of voices rises up around her.

Glory, glory, glory, Lord God Almighty.

It's a moving melody that lifts Flare's spirit. She is one with this group, this room full of strangers only a week ago. She is one with the body of Christ.

And she knows it'll be all right.

When the food has been served and plates devoid of fried chicken, mashed potatoes and corn are pushed away from the edges of the tables, Mr. Deal stands at his seat behind the cross and moves around in front of it. He clinks his glass to get the room's attention.

A deathly silence falls.

"Friends, faculty, students of Heaventree, let me say how proud I am of all of you for what you've accomplished this week. Let us go to God and give praise where praise is due. Dear Heavenly Father, you are the builder of all things. We praise you for your goodness, for your provision, for your shelter. Thank you for watching over us, for keeping these students relatively safe over the long week. We have watched houses built from the ground up, not only the physical buildings but the communities that raised them. Thank you for building us up as your body. Give us the strength and perseverance to withstand any obstacle that comes in our path. Walk with us, lead us, build up our faith and let us not stumble. In Jesus' name. Amen."

The room says, "Amen."

Mr. Deal begins to pace in front of the cross. "It has been my true pleasure getting to know you all this week. Watching you grow together in teams, houses. I suppose there's no way around the fact that our challenge to you was this: whichever house was not finished by week's end would sleep in tents for the duration. Well. Would anyone like to guess who came in last?"

The room is silent, but all eyes seem to fall on Flare's table. She knows what she must do. Slowly, she stands.

"Mr. Deal," says Flare, "it's my house. The House of Flare. It's my fault, really."

Amy reaches over and grabs Flare's hand. Then she stands next to her. They all stand. Together.

Mr. Deal is silent for a few moments as a hush spreads. Finally he says, "You ladies can all take your seats now. Go on. Sit down."

They sit, and Flare takes a deep breath, preparing herself.

"You are right to assume that your house is not finished. I believe you are the only ones who did not achieve electricity, although you did come a long way from day one. In fact, I don't think I am mistaken when I say that your house was helped by several of the other houses. Correct?"

"Yes, sir," says Flare.

"And you still didn't finish?" He says the words with a high-pitched teasing tone.

Flare can't help but smile, and she puts her hand in shame over her reddening face. The room giggles.

"House of Flare, *now* you can stand."

Flare grits her teeth and stares around at her friends as they all rise.

"Ladies, the loser of this week's construction challenge is...the House...of Atlys."

Gasps erupt and everyone looks around themselves, finally resting on a dumbfounded Atlys.

She stands slowly. "Sir?" she says.

"Atlys, although you managed to build your house and add plumbing and electricity per the plans, you neglected one important fact. We are a family here. We are the body of Christ. When Flare broke her arm, the other houses all chipped in to help her house catch up. Your house did not. So even though the electricity is not on in the House of Flare, it appears there is, indeed, Light there. Heaventree is about much more than completing tasks and winning competitions. I should hope that after this event, this is a lesson you will take to heart. Therefore, House of Flare, you may be seated. You have not lost this challenge. House of Atlys, if you would please stand."

The girls in the House of Atlys look utterly destroyed. No one was expecting this. Atlys is now silently crying, rubbing her eyes behind her red glasses. They each stand, one by one.

But the House of Flare remains standing. Slowly, each

of the houses stand. Cornelius, Marcus, Josh, and Nattie. In a few moments, the entire room is standing.

"Order, order," says Mr. Vollmer, standing at his seat and raising his hand.

"Mr. Deal," says Flare. "If I may?"

"You may."

"With all due respect, we have become a family here. And every family has disagreements. But we're in this together, right? If the House of Atlys has to sleep in tents, then so will the House of Flare."

"And so will the House of Josh," says Josh.

"And Nattie."

"And Marcus."

"And Cornelius," says Cornelius, returning his sister's smile.

"I see," says Mr. Deal. He sets his microphone down and walks behind the cross to confer with the other mentors. After a minute, he returns, joined by Mr. Vollmer who says, "You may all be seated."

This time, the room obeys.

"Jesus once told some Pharisees, 'If a house is divided against itself, it cannot stand.' This is true here as well," says Mr. Vollmer. "We are all the House of Heaventree. Together we stand, divided, we fall."

"So true, Mr. Vollmer," says Mr. Deal. "Friends, since I was first given the vision to begin this school, I have trusted in the Lord to guide my decisions. At times, they seem crazy, I'll admit. I didn't know how this construction week would turn out; I only knew it's what the Lord was asking of me. And now I see He was right. You have built yourself into one body. Strike that. The Lord has built you into one body, His body. You are brothers and sisters now. We must work together, depend on one another, look out for each other. You have surprised me and surpassed my expectations for you. And so in my book, there are no losers in this group. Not one."

Atlys sniffs, and the girl beside her hugs her in relief.

"House of Atlys, you have been saved by the sacrifices of your friends. Please remember that. So tonight, I want you each to go to your comfortable beds and have sweet dreams and restful sleep. Tomorrow is a new day. A new challenge will begin." Mr. Deal looks quickly over to Mr. Vollmer, then back at each of the students. His gaze travels to each of their faces as if soaking them all in. He stops when he gets to Cornelius. There, his gaze lingers. He clears his throat.

"Very well, then. Heaventree...you are DISMISSED!"

The students erupt into roars and shouts of joy as hugs go all around and high fives. The House of Flare is elated and still in disbelief, but the House of Atlys has been shaken, and heads hanging, they file back to Chizoba Hall in near silence.

Flare finds Cornelius and hugs him hard with her left arm. "Can you believe it? Isn't it great news? Nobody lost!"

He smiles unconvincingly.

"Aren't you happy?"

"Yeah. Totally happy. Thrilled."

"Okay, well, you seem a little...less than thrilled."

"It's just been a long day, I guess. I'm tired."

"It's been a long *week*. Yeah. Let's go get some sleep," says Flare.

"Sleep. Right. See you in the morning." Cornelius walks ahead of her toward Chizoba Hall with his hands in his pockets. She knows her brother, and something's not right with him. But she'll wait to see what it is in the morning. Right now, she's planning some celebratory rest with a soft pillow, no nurses or infirmary smell, and a decent roof over her head.

~ 27 ~

Cornelius can't sleep. He turns over to his left side and looks at the wall. Tomorrow, everyone at Heaventree will find out their new challenge, whatever that is. They'll also hear about the war going on outside the walls of Heaventree. Cornelius imagines the look on his sister's face when she learns the bad news with the rest of the student body. He doesn't want that to happen. He wants to prepare her. Should he prepare her? HOW can he prepare her? He flips over to his right side. His eyes pop open. It's hopeless. There's no sleeping tonight.

Cornelius hears the soft snoring of his roommate Joe. He sits up quietly and hangs his feet over the bed to touch the floor. He's got to talk to Flare. She needs to hear it from him. So he can hug her. And...well, Cornelius could use a hug right now. He's worried about his parents, and he misses them. He remembers his sister reading Scripture while Pepper was dying, *Yea, though I walk thought the valley of the shadow of death, I will fear no evil...*

He grabs his hoodie, belt and shoes and quietly opens the door, closing it softly behind him so Joe can dream on in peace. Then he heads toward the elevator to find Flare.

At first, there's no answer. Of course, there isn't. It's close to midnight. Flare's finally resting without a care in the world—she doesn't have to sleep in a tent. Cornelius grabs his stomach. He knocks again. Finally, the door cracks open.

Please be Flare. Please be Flare.

"What are you doing?" Flare's whispers groggily. "I was sleeping."

"I know. I'm sorry, I just...we need to talk."

Flare stares into his eyes, sees he's serious, then nods and shuts the door. When she opens it again she's dressed in jeans and a pullover, her hand tucked in the front pocket. Brother and sister walk in silence to the elevator. Flare is about the push the button when Cornelius changes his mind. "Let's take the stairs instead."

Down and down they go, around and around until they see the number 2 next to a doorway. Cornelius descends a little further and then sits mid-flight. Flare takes a place on the stair beneath him. The walls here are concrete and bleak with shadows. They seem to be closing in on him. There is nothing in here that reminds them of Heaventree. This could be a stairwell in any building in the world. But it's not. It's here. At Heaventree. And now he has to tell his sister the truth about this place.

"Well?" says Flare.

Cornelius knows he needs to talk to her, but now he's unsure of what to say, exactly.

"Mr. Deal," spills out of his mouth. "He's not what we think he is."

"What do you mean?"

"I mean...he's a good guy, but...that's just it. He used to be a GUY."

"No way."

"Way. I've seen his scar. I talked to him about it. He used to be a GUY. He cut out his own chip."

Flare swallows. Cornelius can see the anxiety in her eyes. He knows what she's thinking. If Mr. Deal was a GUY, then maybe this whole Heaventree thing is a trap.

"So what does this mean?" says Flare, slowly, steeling herself.

"It means he knows what he's talking about. He knows how the GUYs think. He understands so much more than we do. He had the whole Bible downloaded into his brain and every other religious text there is. He's a believer, a Christ-follower, Flare, trust me on that."

Flare studies him for a moment, then hauls back and punches him in the arm.

"Ow!"

"Why didn't you tell me?"

"It's been a busy week," says Cornelius, holding his bicep.

"I know, but seriously, something like that—"

"That's not even what I wanted to talk about."

"It's not? Well, what then? What could possibly be more—"

"There's a war going on. Outside of Heaventree. Mr. Deal told me all about it. Those without the mark are being...hunted."

"Hunted? What do you mean? Mom and Dad?"

Cornelius nods, never taking his eyes off of hers. "Yeah.

He said we were brought here just in time for prophecy to be fulfilled."

"Prophecy. You mean dad's dream about the dog, about Pepper dying..."

"Yeah. All those parents and grandparents had dreams, visions...they were all pointed to this school, something Mr. Deal was moved to create a long time ago."

"And so we're here, doing what...being protected while Mom and Dad are...are...my God, are they even alive?" She puts her hands over her mouth and her eyes grow large.

"I hope so."

The two are quiet for what seems like eternity, Flare staring at her shoes, Cornelius staring at her backs of her hands covered in ink.

"You've been drawing again."

"Yeah, well." She sniffs. "I thought I was happy here, for once. I did it in prayer for Miss Carmine. Oh my gosh, Miss Carmine! Now it all makes sense! No wonder she's hurt!"

"No, it doesn't all make sense. We still don't know why she was out there in the first place, do we? I mean, she was your mentor. Why wasn't she here, helping you build your house?"

"I don't know, but...wait a minute." Flare stands so quickly, she nearly topples. "The book."

"The book?" says Cornelius.

She grabs him by the shirt. "Yes, don't you see? That book has something to do with this. I know it does. And Amy's parents' names were written in the book."

"Yeah, but what does that mean?"

"No clue. But I know who does," says Flare. "Deal knows what that book is. He knows all of this. Everything about this place. This was his vision, you know."

"I...I guess."

Flare grabs Cornelius' arm and starts running down the stairs.

"Wait? Where are we going?" cries Cornelius.

"To see Deal," says Flare with that authoritative big sister voice she gets when she's being bossy and nothing will change her mind. With everything in him, Cornelius wants to stop her, to stop them, but he knows it's no use. Instead, he succumbs and begins running alongside her out of Chizoba Hall and quietly into the dark of night. He prays he won't regret this. Part of him still feels wary of Mr. Deal. He was a GUY after all. But the other part of Cornelius, his deep hidden faith, understands that Mr. Deal knows much more than he's let on. Will he be angry getting woken up in the middle of the night? Cornelius is going to have to handle the consequences of telling Mr. Deal's secret, but then again, Mr. Deal's going to have to handle Flare's questions and wrath.

Cornelius sort of pities him.

~ 28 ~

In the moonlight, Castlebank looks ominous, a looming jagged shadow. Flare takes a deep breath and grabs her brother's hand. "It'll be locked, so we'll have to try the window I went in before," she whispers. She expects some sort of resistance from Corn, but gets none. He's going along willingly, which only amplifies the fact that all of this is very serious. The war outside is real.

Flare and Corn crawl behind the bushes and inch their way left, away from the front door. There's no light on in the window like there was the last time. The only lights on are on the sixth floor. Maybe that's where Mr. Deal is. Awake still.

"Here it is." Flare pushes on the tall narrow window she went in the last time. Thankfully, it gives. "Okay, I'll go first. Give me a hand."

Flare hoists herself up on the sill while Corn pushes her legs up. Once inside, she says, "Your turn." When they're both inside the dark room, she pulls the window shut. Total silence envelopes them, but her heart is beating like crazy.

"Before we find Deal, I want you to see the book."

"Are you sure about this?"

Flare responds by grabbing his arm and pulling. With her other arm, she feels her way in the dark toward where she hopes the door is.

Thump!

She hits something. A lamp? She reaches wildly and keeps it from falling over. When she knows it's standing upright, she clutches at her heart. That was too close!

In a minute or two, their eyes acclimate to the darkness and she can easily see the hallway. "This way."

They tiptoe across the stone floors down to the left. Flare stops when she gets to a door. On either side of it are stained glass windows. She can barely see some red and yellow from the moonlight coming from the other side. She tries the doorknob.

"It's locked. I can't believe this."

"Maybe we shouldn't be here," says Corn. "Maybe we should just talk to Mr. Deal in the morning. I think we should go."

"No, we can't go! We're already here. We're this close."

"But the door is locked."

"Yeah, it is." She feels around. "And there doesn't seem to be a keyhole." Flare shuts her eyes for a minute and calms her breathing. Think, Flare. Lord, how do we get in this room? She opens her eyes. She has an idea. "There are two stained glass windows on either side of this door. I remember they they're Biblical scenes. Here. See if we can figure out what they are."

"It's too dark. You'll have to turn on a light."

"I don't want to do that. Not yet. Look. Bend down

like this and try to catch the moonlight. I'll study this one and you look at that one." Flare kneels down and uses the moonlight from the rose window inside the room to illuminate the stained glass window, piece by piece, as she moves her body. She sees reds, yellows, greens, blues, purples. Finally, she whispers, "It's a scene from Revelation. From the end times. It's the throne of God with the river like glass before it. Can you figure out yours yet?"

"I, I think so. Wait," says Corn. "Yeah, I think this one is from Genesis. It's Creation, God creating the heavens and earth."

"Okay," says Flare, her mind churning. "Genesis and Revelation. The beginning and the end. What is it, 'I am the Alpha and Omega...'"

"That's it," says Corn. "I am the Alpha and the Omega, the First and the Last, the Beginning and the End."

They hear a click.

"Try it now," says Corn. Flare turns the knob, and unbelievably, it opens. She leans over and hugs him quietly, trying to contain her excitement.

They're in.

"Right here in the middle," whispers Flare. "Here's the book."

"It's huge," says Corn.

Flare opens it slowly and carefully lays the cover down. It's dark in the room, but strangely the pages seem to glow. Cornelius moves closer to his sister. "I see the words, but nothing's changing."

"Wait. Watch this." Flare turns the pages until she gets further toward the back. "Yep, here's Amy's parents' names. See? I told you. Wow, a lot of names have been added since I was in here last. And look, the dates are progressing too. Okay. Here's the last name. Simon Everett Fowl. The date is yesterday."

"Flare," says Corn, gravely.

"Yeah."

"Did you see it? Look."

Flare moves her eyes to where Corn is pointing on the other page.

"Miss Carmine? Why is Miss Carmine's name in here?"

Corn is quiet. So is Flare. Why would her mentor's name be in here? What is this book?

"I thought you said the book writes itself," Corn says finally. "I don't see any of that happening."

"I don't know. I promise it did. I was here, just looking, and then—"

"Sh!" Corn leans in closer to the pages. "Do you hear that?"

There is a scratching sound. Barely perceptible, but there, nonetheless. Black lines begin to etch into the page below the last name. It's a slow calligraphy as if a human hand is writing with a feather quill and ink.

Anna Claire Fowl

"It's dated today. Right now," says Corn. "This book is showing what's happening to Anna Claire Fowl right now."

An uneasy fear takes over them. Flare turns the pages back.

"What are you doing?

"Looking for our names. Or mom's and dad's."

Silently, Flare and Cornelius set to the slow and tedious task. When they've gone back nearly ten years, the sun is threatening to come up.

"We've got to go," says Flare. "We have to see Mr. Deal before breakfast." She takes the cover and slowly closes the book, feeling the jewels on top. She knows the book is special, sacred, but she just can't be sure of what it is. Flare doesn't believe in magic. She does believe in God. It's this that carries her, humbled and in awe that she's on to something really important.

~ 29 ~

Cornelius and Flare creep down the hallway toward the main entrance of Castlebank. They find a stairwell next to the elevator and make it all the way to Mr. Deal's floor out of eye sight. And out of breath. Stealth is exhausting. Cornelius is sweating. He wipes away his hair from his brow.

Cornelius sticks his head out of the door and looks down the hallway. Coach Arnold, Josh's mentor, is walking toward him. What is he doing up this early? Cornelius jerks his head back and shuts the door quietly. He holds his breath, pressing his head to the wall and praying Coach Arnold didn't see him. When the footsteps pass, he thinks he's home free.

"This won't be easy," he tells his sister.

Flare nods.

Cornelius puts up his hand and counts on three fingers. 1-2-3. He opens the door and crawls out into the hallway. They run like this, hunched over, until they get to Mr. Deal's room. The light is on under his door.

Tap-tap-tap.

Cornelius can feel his blood pumping.

Tap-tap-tap-tap.

After a couple more seconds, the doorknob turns. Mr. Deal's face appears, confused at first, then recognition settles in and something else. He grabs Cornelius and pulls him in, Flare following close behind.

"What are you two doing here?"

"I—well, we—" Cornelius looks back at his sister for the words.

"Corn told me everything. He told me about the war going on outside Heaventree. He told me how our families are being hunted. He told me you used to be a GUY. And now I need some answers."

Mr. Deal looks sternly at Cornelius. His eyes narrow.

Exasperated, Cornelius says, "You don't understand. She pulled it out of me."

"You cannot have things pulled out of you!" Deal bangs his hand on a table and raises his voice. Then quieting down he says, "You promised you wouldn't say anything. A man is nothing without his word."

"My brother is a better man than you are!" says Flare, crossing her arms.

Cornelius looks back at her stunned. Scared.

Mr. Deal breathes heavily and turns around. "Perhaps you are right about that," he mumbles. He goes to a chair and pulls it out. Then another. He sits across from them and motions for them to have a seat. "I guess there's no more time for secrets. It's all going to be out soon."

"Mr. Deal," says Flare diplomatically, "it has come to our attention that there exists a book, a special book here in Castlebank, filled with names and dates." She watches his eyes to see how he reacts. He doesn't.

"This book, I have it on good authority, seems to write itself. And there are names I recognize, er, one would recognize. Those of Amy Feinstein's parents in particular, and more recently...Miss Carmine."

Cornelius bites his lip. Mr. Deal takes his hands and folds them under his chin. He closes his eyes for a moment, as if praying, and then opens them and leans forward.

"You two are amazing," he says. "Who else knows about the book?"

"No one," says Flare. "Just us."

He sighs. "Good. We need to keep it that way."

"Why?" says Cornelius. "What is it?"

"It's the oldest book there is. As old as the battle of good and evil itself."

"Older than the Bible? What, the book of life?" says Corn, snickering and looking at his sister.

"The book of life, no," says Deal. "But an important book nonetheless. The book is a living document and is still being written. We call it the Book of Martyrs."

"The book of martyrs," says Flare, "Then that means that, that..."

"That martyrs' names are written in it," answers Deal. "From the beginning of time, people who have lost their lives because of their faith in God have had their names written there. It is not an earthly book, I assure you. It's a sacred book. It's said the hand of an angel inscribes each and every martyr."

Flare stands up. "But that means Amy's parents are...dead?" Her eyes widen.

"Flare," says Cornelius, "It also means Miss Carmine..."

"No," whimpers Flare. She plops back down in the chair.

"Miss Carmine succumbed to her injuries last night, Flare," says Mr. Deal. "I'm sorry."

"But why is she a martyr?" asks Cornelius.

"She was performing a grave and dangerous task for Heaventree when a bomb fell. She was unconscious when she was found but still alive."

"But why was she out there?" says Flare, standing again. "Why was she out there and not in here, being my mentor? Why would you send her out there if you knew a war was going on? Why couldn't you send someone else?"

"There was no one else who could do what she could do. Miss Carmine is...was...a phenomenally gifted artist. She was responsible for keeping Heaventree hidden from the rest of the world. She painted, if you will, the camouflage around our campus."

"Painted? But I don't understand. I did wonder how we couldn't see this place, even when we were right at the gate."

"Miss Carmine didn't paint with colors seen with the human eye. She was entrusted with a heavenly palette. Her artistry was her faith. She literally painted us invisible with faith and prayers. The night she was hurt, she was touching up some cracks. The dome requires regular maintenance. And now, without her here, I'm afraid we're vulnerable to holes opening up."

Cornelius and Flare try to take this all in. They pace

the room. Their minds are blown. First there was talk of the Book of Martrys with an angel writing the names of the dead. And then there was this faith-painted dome of invisibility over Heaventree. It's hard to fathom, even harder to accept as truth.

Finally, Cornelius says, "So if Miss Carmine isn't here to maintain the dome, that means it's going to fail at some point. I mean, we won't remain hidden here at Heaventree. The GU will find us here."

"They will, yes," says Mr. Deal. "If no one maintains the dome. But I believe there may be an answer to prayer on that. We may have found someone who can do exactly what Miss Carmine was doing."

"Well, who is it?" says Flare, freaked now.

Mr. Deal gets up from his chair and walks toward her. He puts his hands on her shoulders and squares her to him, eye to eye. "I believe that person is you, Flare."

She pulls away. "Me? What do I know about it? I don't know how to do what she was doing, painting invisible things."

"Not yet, no, but...she left you some things."

Mr. Deal walks to his bureau and opens up a drawer. Inside is a large manila envelope marked *Personal effects of Miss Amelia Carmine.* He hands the envelope to Flare. "Everyone will be getting new assignments this morning after breakfast. This, dear girl, is yours."

Flare takes the envelope in her hands and feels the weight of it, rubbing it in her fingers. She looks to her brother then.

"And me?" says Cornelius. "I'm almost afraid to ask,

Mr. Deal. But what is my new assignment? To help Flare with the camouflage?"

Mr. Deal turns and walks to the window. He stands there for a moment. "The sun is coming up soon. I can see the barest hint of light. Beautiful."

Cornelius swallows. He can't speak. Normally a straight shooter, Mr. Deal is obviously stalling. Flare and Cornelius stand and clasp hands. They watch Mr. Deal's head fall as he turns back to face them. Finally, their eyes meet.

"Cornelius, I know you may find all of this hard to believe, but I knew it the moment I met you. Yes, I know you're anxious and more comfortable taking a back seat role. But God has other plans for you. You see, when all of those people around the world began to have visions of this school and of sending their children here, they had visions of me, yes. But there was another part of the prophecy. A very unlikely soul, a timid young man with great wisdom, would lead our saints on R & R missions."

"I hope that means rest and relaxation," says Cornelius.

"Not quite. Reconnaissance and rescue. We're sending you to the battlefields."

"The battlefields? Cornelius?" says Flare incredulously, pulling him even tighter.

"I mean that figuratively, or course. At this point, no place but Heaventree is safe, so outside these walls....Listen. I will share your new mission with you in a couple of hours when we are all together as one body, but suffice it to say, we will have reason to leave Heaventree, and it will be extremely dangerous. You won't go it alone, but you will have great responsibility. You have been faithful with what you've been given so far...well, you know how the verse goes."

"For the one who has been entrusted with much, much more will be asked."

"Exactly," says Mr. Deal. He moves forward and puts his arm on Cornelius's shoulder. "If I can give you any encouragement now, understand that God uses unlikely people to accomplish his mightiest acts so that no man can boast. Look at me, for instance. A former GUY now running his school."

"That's true," says Cornelius.

"And do you know how many times the phrase, 'Do not be afraid,' or something like it is used in Scripture?"

"You know I do."

"Then I suggest you bring it all to mind now as you're about to lead your friends into grave danger, and you're going to need all the courage you can muster."

Mr. Deal walks to the door and opens it. "I'll see you after breakfast. Be sure to eat a hearty meal, and don't let on that you know anything. We need our students strong and refreshed."

The door closes behind Mr. Deal, leaving Flare and Cornelius standing in silence, their hearts thumping in tandem. As they think over everything that Mr. Deal has just handed them, a thought seems to strike them at the very same moment. Their heads rise and they stare wide-eyed and whisper, "Reconnaissance and *rescue*?"

Each sibling understands what this means, so they hug each other tight with trepidation...and just the slightest bit of hope that their parents are still alive.

With Flare and Cornelius safely out of the room, Mr. Deal wipes his brow and sits at his desk. He opens a drawer and lifts out a tattered old laptop that contains the chip he pulled from his own forehead. He opens the screen and finds an urgent message being downloaded this moment into GUYs all over the world.

... G.O.D. new directive/status: immediate/
... All pets must now be chipped and connected to a new G.O.D. link especially suited to animals ... In addition, all pets of enemies of the state, non-G.U.Y.s, who have eluded elimination, must be confiscated ... Unless posing direct physical threat, these animals are not to be harmed ... It has been observed that unchipped pets exhibit a strong loyalty and protection to their owners ... The Global Union has use for these creatures in tracking down non-G.U.Y.s, now classified as a VIRUS to the G.O.D. ... The virus must be cleansed from the system. ... Cleanse the virus from the system.

Mr. Deal closes his eyes and rubs his throbbing head. Slowly he stands and walks toward the window where he can see the past week's construction and the six houses of Heaventree standing tall.

"As usual, Lord, you have tipped me off and kept us one step ahead of them," he says. "Thank you, Father. And watch over your children, for their next assignment will be much harder than the last."

ABOUT THE AUTHOR

The Firstborn is Nicole Seitz' first YA novel, the first in the *House of Heaventree* series. She is the acclaimed author of seven other novels and two non-fiction anthologies for adults. She teaches visual art, creative writing and illustration at a school in the Charleston, SC area where she lives with her husband and two children. Seitz is a graduate of the University of North Carolina at Chapel Hill's School of Journalism and also has a degree in Illustration from Savannah College of Art & Design. Her paintings are featured on the covers of her books. Visit her web site at www.nicoleseitz.com for more information.

ALSO BY NICOLE SEITZ

YA Fiction

The Virus (House of Heaventree, Book 2 - Stay tuned for Book 3!)

Adult Fiction

The Cage-maker
Beyond Molasses Creek
The Inheritance of Beauty
Saving Cicadas
A Hundred Years of Happiness
Trouble the Water
The Spirit of Sweetgrass

Adult Non-fiction

When You Pass Through Waters: Words of Hope and Healing from Your Favorite Authors
Our Prince of Scribes: Writers Remember Pat Conroy (coeditor)